SUMMER HOUSE MYSTERY

THE MYSTERY HOUSE SERIES, BOOK ELEVEN

Eva Pohler

Copyright © 2023 by Eva Pohler.

All rights reserved. No part of this publication may be reproduced, distributed or transmitted in any form or by any means, including photocopying, recording, or other electronic or mechanical methods, without the prior written permission of the publisher, except in the case of brief quotations embodied in critical reviews and certain other noncommercial uses permitted by copyright law. For permission requests, write to the publisher, addressed "Attention: Permissions Coordinator," at the address below.

Eva Pohler Books
20011 Park Ranch
San Antonio, Texas 78259
www.evapohler.com

Publisher's Note: This is a work of fiction. Names, characters, places, and incidents are a product of the author's imagination. Locales and public names are sometimes used for atmospheric purposes. Any resemblance to actual people, living or dead, or to businesses, companies, events, institutions, or locales is completely coincidental.

Copy Editor: Alexis Rigoni

Book Cover Design by B Rose DesignZ

SUMMER HOUSE MYSTERY/ Eva Pohler. -- 1st ed.
ISBN: 9798399999326

Contents

The Bones 3
The Summer House 12
Biloxi Beach 22
Mary Mahoney's Old French House 32
Mixed Messages 44
Biloxi Lighthouse 55
The Third Floor 67
The Box 76
The Sherry Murders 89
Sisters of Mercy 100
A Saturday Night Séance 114
The Golden Key 123
Mr. Mike 132
Mr. Mike's Daughter 139
The Biloxi Orphanage 147
The Wait 154
On the Run 163
Gulfport-Biloxi International Airport 172
Dog Trouble 179
The Man in the Mask 188
Devious Minds 197
More Trouble 206

The El Reno Correction Facility 219
Return to Biloxi 227
Acknowledgments 234

For the victims of the Dixie Mafia and their families.

CHAPTER ONE

The Bones

It was late when Ellen and her friends and her little dog, Moseby, arrived at the Inn on Ursulines in the French Quarter of New Orleans on a hot summer night. They had just checked in and were in the courtyard heading toward their suite when Tanya's phone rang.

"It's Priestess Isabel," Tanya, the tallest and thinnest of the three friends, said as she put the phone to her ear. "Hello, Priestess . . . isn't it a bit late for that tonight? . . . Okay, hold on a sec." Tanya cupped a hand over the phone as her long, blonde ponytail blew in the evening breeze. "She wants us to come tonight. It's already past nine. What do you think?"

Ellen had gone ahead a few paces to insert her key card into the door. "I'm tired from the flight, but if that's what she wants."

"She said she's unavailable in the morning," Tanya explained.

"We better go tonight, then," Sue agreed as she followed Ellen inside. "If we want to throw the bones ourselves."

"Okay, Priestess," Tanya said into the phone. "We'll see you soon."

"On the way, we can grab coffee and pastries to share with her," Ellen suggested when Tanya appeared in the doorway. "Maybe that will wake us up."

Sue grinned. "Now, you're singing my song."

Fifteen minutes later, they arrived at the Voodoo Spiritual Temple on North Rampart via their rental car—a blue Honda Pilot—and entered Priestess Isabel's establishment. The scent of lavender and roses permeated the air, immediately soothing and relaxing Ellen. From the back of the crowded shop full of Voodoo dolls, *gris gris* bags, sachets, incense, charms, and other paraphernalia, Priestess Isabel appeared wearing a smile.

Tanya greeted her with a coffee.

"Well, isn't that nice," the priestess said.

"We brought pastries, too." Sue, the shortest and the plumpest, opened the lid on the bakery box to show off the goods. "Hope you're hungry."

"Welcome, ladies." The petite priestess was nearly as short as Sue with black, tight curls that were close to her head. "Who's this?" she asked of the dog.

"Moseby," Ellen, who was the middle one of the three friends in height, weight, and politics, cradled him in his cloth pooch carrier.

The little, black dog opened his eyes and looked at the priestess before closing them again.

"He doesn't find me very interesting." Isabel laughed as she beckoned them to follow her. "Let's go out back."

She led them to the courtyard, where the light breeze did nothing to alter the sultry evening air. "Who's throwing first?"

"I will." Sue laid the bakery box on the stone retaining wall that surrounded Isabel's herb and flower garden. Then she took a seat at the bistro table and picked up the dried bones, shells, and rocks that were scattered across the woven mat. "I need to know about my heart palpitations. Should I be worried? The doctor thinks I'm overreacting."

Isabel took a seat across from Sue. "Give them a shake."

"I really don't want to go on any more medication, if I can avoid it," Sue added. "I already feel like every time I try to pronounce the medications I'm taking, I may be summoning a demon instead."

Ellen and Tanya laughed as they watched Sue throw the bones.

Isabel studied the lay of each of the items on the mat. "Are you drinking too much caffeine? These indicate an addiction. How much coffee and soda do you consume?"

"Well," Sue began with a frown. "I like to start my day with a caramel mocha latte, and by lunch time, I start craving my cherry coke."

"You might want to cut out one of those," Isabel said, eyeing the Styrofoam cup of coffee Sue had put to her lips.

Sue lifted her brows. "What? I don't drink nearly as much caffeine as other people I know. Are you sure that's what the bones say?"

"Are you questioning my abilities? If you don't like what I have to say, don't ask."

"It could be worse," Tanya pointed out. "You were worried you might need an ablation."

Sue pushed her brown bangs from her equally brown eyes. "I'm sorry. I'm not questioning you, Priestess. I just can't bear to part with my two favorite drinks. Who wants to go next?"

"You don't have to part with them," Isabel clarified. "Just cut down."

"We all know how good I am at depriving myself." Sue climbed from the chair and leaned against the stone retaining wall as Tanya and Ellen each offered the other one the chair.

"Go ahead," Ellen insisted.

Tanya took a seat and gathered up the bones before shaking them and throwing them across the mat.

"What's your question?" the priestess asked.

"Should I gamble at the casinos while I'm here? Or will it be a waste of money?"

Isabel leaned over the table to study the layout. "The bones promise riches and surprising discoveries in the coming days."

Tanya clapped her hands. "Yay! That's exciting!"

"Beau Rivage, here we come!" Ellen cheered.

Sue rolled her eyes and mumbled, "Can Tanya and I trade readings?"

Isabel laughed at Sue. "Friend, you need the opposite of caffeine. You're so tense and stressed, I can feel it. Let me make you my special tea to calm your nerves."

"What are you stressed about, Sue?" Ellen asked.

"Oh, I don't know. We'll talk about it later."

Ellen and Tanya exchanged looks of concern. Ellen decided to let it go for now, not wanting to press for more information in front of the priestess.

Ellen switched places with Tanya and gathered the shells, bones, and rocks. As she shook them in her hands, she asked, "Will Lane and Maya's baby be a girl or a boy?"

Then she threw the objects across the table and waited eagerly as Isabel studied them.

"All signs point to feminine energy," the priestess finally said. "I see a baby girl in your future."

Ellen straightened her back. "I knew it! That's exactly what I told Lane."

"Maybe *you* should become a priestess," Sue teased.

Ellen winked at Isabel. "Maybe I should."

A half hour later, they sat inside Isabel's sitting room next door to her shop, chatting over tea and pastries. Surrounded by artifacts from all over the world, including dolls, pottery, tapestries, costumes, beads, an old organ, masks, horns, and other oddities, many which were stuffed with one-dollar bills, the priestess rambled about the illusions people have of one another. Ellen, who felt sleepy and content, had begun to suspect that there were more than black tea leaves in her brew.

"We all have illusions," Sue agreed, her lids half closed. "My marriage depends on them."

Ellen chuckled, but when the priestess blurted out a hysterical cackle, Ellen's laughter became uncontrollable. Her rib cage hurt, and she peed a little.

"Oh, no!" Ellen cried. "I just wet myself!"

She and her friends laughed even harder.

"What's in this tea, Priestess?" Tanya asked.

"Just hemp leaves," she said. "It's the best antidote to stress. You ladies needed this."

"You got us high?" Ellen cried through her giggles. "How will we drive ourselves home?"

"It's only a ten-minute walk to the inn from here," Isabel pointed out. "Or you can Uber."

"Who would have thought that 'uber' would become one of the most used verbs in the English language?" Sue reflected. "It's such a funny sounding word."

The other three friends each said 'uber' repeatedly, laughing at the way it sounded.

"It sounds like rubber," Ellen pointed out. "Another funny word."

"And such a funny thing, too," Tanya noted. "A dick sleeve. It's strange what humans think up, isn't it?"

Another wave of hysteria swept over Ellen at the mention of "dick sleeve," especially from Tanya, who rarely said anything vulgar.

"I peed again!" Ellen cried, standing up. "I don't want to wet your chair, Priestess."

"That chair has seen worse," Isabel said with a chuckle.

Ellen and Tanya exchanged glances. An image of the priestess getting down with a lover on the furniture entered Ellen's mind. Tanya must have had a similar vision because they both busted out laughing.

"Do you need to use the restroom?" Tanya asked Ellen after a beat.

"I think I'm done now," Ellen admitted.

"Will this tea be good for my heart palpitations?" Sue asked Isabel. "I feel pretty relaxed, to tell you the truth."

"Absolutely," Isabel confirmed. "It will also help with your visions, which you're going to need in Biloxi."

"Why would you say that?" Tanya wanted to know.

"I have a feeling," the priestess explained. "I'm sure there's someone there who will want to talk to you."

"Really?" Ellen asked. "Maybe I should throw the bones again."

The priestess set her teacup on the coffee table and stood up. "Let's go."

They filed out of the building into the courtyard, where Tanya and Sue watched as Ellen shook the bones. "Will we encounter ghosts in Biloxi?" She dropped them across the mat.

Priestess Isabel took a long look, her brow furrowed.

"What do they say?" Ellen asked impatiently.

Isabel scratched her head. "This may not make any sense, but they indicate something about a boundary. There's a line you shouldn't cross, a place you shouldn't enter. One part of the house you're staying at might be dangerous. You should be able to feel it as soon as you go inside. Just avoid that room or that part of the house, and you'll be fine."

Tanya's face sobered. "What if we *don't* feel it? What if we enter the dangerous side?"

"I'll pack you some of my special tea bags to take with you," Isabel said. "It relaxes the body and sharpens the sixth sense."

Because Ellen's pants were damp, she convinced the others to walk the six blocks from the Voodoo Spiritual Temple to the Inn on Ursulines. Moseby hadn't needed convincing, happy to escape his cloth pooch carrier to stroll on his leash in front of them. Sue, who seemed more relaxed than ever, didn't complain about her feet as she ambled along between Ellen and Tanya, chatting about their upcoming luck at the casinos and the impending arrival of Ellen's grandbaby girl. The streets were crowded with tourists, many of whom were on ghost tours. Ellen tried to listen in on what one of the guides was saying about Delphine LaLaurie, but Sue's chatter drowned out the other voice.

"Almost everything she said tonight was positive," Sue noted. "It was worth flying into New Orleans to see her, don't you think? I mean, I suppose I can alternate between my caramel mocha lattes and my cherry cokes. I don't have to give them up—just cut back. Maybe the doctor was right about my not needing an ablation. I'm glad I got a second opinion, anyway. And the drive to Biloxi tomorrow will be a breeze."

"Well, the one negative thing was a biggie," Tanya argued. "Wouldn't you agree, Ellen?"

Ellen laughed. "It's just a very small thing that our Biloxi home rental has a dangerous side, and our best defense against it seems to be hemp tea!"

"If you plan to drink more of it on this trip," Sue said to Ellen, "it might be time to invest in adult diapers."

The three friends laughed hysterically as they continued their walk in the sultry night through the French Quarter.

CHAPTER TWO

The Summer House

The next morning, Tanya and Ellen strolled through the French Quarter with Moseby to the Voodoo Spiritual Temple to retrieve their rental car before picking up Sue and heading out to Biloxi, Mississippi. In a little over an hour, they reached the palatial, white house on Beach Boulevard that they would call home for the next seven days. It sat on a hill overlooking Biloxi Public Beach and the iconic lighthouse across the street.

As they turned off the main road, Ellen got a closer view of the house. It was a three-story Greek revival at the top of a long hill of green lawn. Steps made of red pavers stretched across the façade with six towering white columns that reached up to a second story balcony, reminding Ellen of the Parthenon. Behind the white railing of the balcony, Ellen could see floor-to-ceiling windows trimmed with black shutters. Above the second floor loomed a large dormer with three tall windows. Ellen found the symmetry of the house—along with the contrast between the white paint, red pavers, and the black roof and shutters—pleasing.

Driving up from a side street, they pulled into the driveway leading to two carriage-style garage doors near the back of the house.

"Is this where I park?" Sue asked Tanya, who sat beside her in the front.

Tanya nodded. "We don't have access to the garage."

Unlike their summer rental, the home behind it faced the side street, and it was small in comparison. A black German shepherd eyed them curiously from the end of a rope tethered to a stake in the front yard. Ellen kept Moseby close in his cloth pooch carrier to avoid a scene. She was surprised when the bigger dog did nothing more than stare at them as they unloaded their luggage.

From the driveway, they followed a path to a side door where a red-paved porch and a black awning were flanked by charming gas-lit lanterns.

Moseby squirmed, so Ellen leashed him and let him sniff the grass while Tanya entered a code into the lockbox.

The side door opened to a narrow hall leading to three other doors. The door to the right, which was locked, led to the garage. The door straight ahead opened onto a large breezeway. Through the glass panes of the door, Ellen could see patio furniture arranged on the red brick pavers to take advantage of the ocean views, and behind it was an outdoor shower off the back of the garage. The door to the left led to a bright stairwell.

Although the space was small, the stairwell felt large with tall windows on two sides looking out to the ocean and onto the breezeway.

Tanya led the way up the stairs, pulling her bag behind her.

"What a gorgeous house in a stunning location," Ellen said as she followed Tanya.

"Be on alert for the supposed dangerous side," Sue, who took up the rear, reminded them, before adding, "Why did you have to pick a place with stairs, Tanya?"

"This is one of the few historical homes on the strip to have survived Hurricanes Camille and Katrina," she explained. "Mainly because it's built to withstand strong winds and floods."

"Safety before convenience," Ellen said with approval as they reached the second floor.

"Though, I don't think we're expecting a hurricane anytime soon," Sue grumbled.

At the second-floor landing, they were greeted by yet another door, which, once opened, led to a beautiful living area with gorgeous views of the ocean and a door to a balcony as wide as the façade of the house.

"Isn't this lovely?" Ellen said as she opened the double French doors to the balcony, where four wooden rockers, a patio table and four chairs, and a porch swing made it the perfect place to take in the view. "I can see us enjoying margaritas out here tonight."

"I love the Victorian-style furnishings," Tanya said of the furniture inside—a curved chaise lounge, wingback chairs, and Queen Anne coffee and end tables.

The chaise lounge was on the same wall as the entrance, while the wingback chairs flanked the fireplace, which had an ornate wooden mantle and façade facing the floor-to-ceiling windows overlooking the gulf. Across the room from the chaise lounge was a round, wooden dining set for four with a television mounted on the wall above it, and to the right of it, just across the room from the entry, was a doorway into a kitchen.

Sue pointed to her feet. "This rug looks expensive, and the floors look as though they were refinished recently."

"They were," Tanya confirmed. "The homeowner told me that the house suffered quite a bit of damage from Hurricane Katrina. She and her husband are still renovating. In fact, she asked us not to go to the third floor, as it's still under construction."

Ellen snapped her fingers. "I bet that's the dangerous side Priestess Isabel warned us about."

"You think there's something evil on the third floor?" Tanya asked Ellen with her brows lifted.

Ellen shrugged. "I'm just saying it could be the area we're meant to avoid."

"That would be convenient, wouldn't it?" Sue smirked as she crossed the living area and into the kitchen. "This is cute. Check out the antique dishes and tins on the open shelving."

Tanya followed. "So, you don't think it's the third floor?"

Sue shrugged. "I didn't say that."

Ellen entered the galley kitchen behind Tanya, admiring the antique tins of Frank's Allspice, Quaker Oats, Old Hickory Pure Lard, Borden's Meadow Brand Malted Milk, Bean Coffee, and General Food's MAX-I-MUM Brand Peanut Butter. A wave of nostalgia swept over Ellen, and she was a little girl standing in her mother's kitchen reaching for the saltines in the old-style tin they used to come in.

"Is this a dumbwaiter?" Tanya said, pointing to what appeared to be exactly that.

Tanya slid open the door and looked down. "I think this goes all the way to the breezeway."

"It sure beats hauling your groceries up the stairs," Sue commented. "Push the button and see if it works."

Tanya pushed the button. They heard a slight buzzing sound as the dumbwaiter ascended from the ground level.

"That sure is neat," Ellen said. "I can't wait to use it after we go shopping."

"I wish we would have known about that before we lugged all our bags up here," Sue complained.

"Well, now we know we can send them down when it's time to leave," Tanya pointed out.

Tanya closed the sliding door and left the kitchen. Sue followed.

"Oh, I want this room," Sue said from another door adjacent to the kitchen. "It's really pretty in here, though there's not much of a view."

"I guess I'll take this one then, if that's alright with you, Ellen," Tanya said of the room next to Sue's. "I'm not getting any negative vibes from it. What about you, Sue?"

"This room seems fine to me," Sue replied. "Are all the ceilings painted in this pretty teal?"

"I think so," Tanya said. "It really is pretty with the white walls and dark wood floors and furnishings."

"There's a bathroom for us to share," Sue pointed out to Tanya as Ellen turned toward the entrance to the bedroom over the garage.

It was next to the guest bathroom, which she supposed she'd have to herself. She glanced inside at the clawfoot tub and pedestal sink before entering the bedroom that was to be hers for the week. It appeared to be larger than the others with a queen—rather than a double—bed, along with a writing desk in one corner. She, too, felt nothing negative or foreboding as she glanced out the back window. The German shepherd lay bored on the front yard of the house below. Ellen felt sorry for him.

"This must be the master," Sue said as she entered. "I guess I jumped the gun."

"Do you want to trade?" Ellen offered, though she'd rather keep the room for herself.

Sue must have sensed Ellen's reluctance. "No, that's okay. I'm fine where I'm at."

They both jumped at the sound of something heavy hitting the floor above them.

"What was that?" Tanya asked as she returned from the kitchen.

Ellen and Sue exchanged looks of alarm.

Sue turned to Tanya. "Did the landlord say there would be workers renovating during our stay?"

"Absolutely not. That would suck."

Ellen agreed. "Maybe one of the owners came by to grab something, not realizing we'd be here by now?"

The three friends returned to the stairwell and looked up, listening quietly for several seconds. Moseby growled, which further alarmed Ellen. When they heard nothing more, they shrugged and returned to their second-floor living room.

"Maybe something fell over," Sue speculated, "something that had been recently moved."

Tanya nodded. "Or maybe there's an animal up there, like a raccoon."

"That's probably all it was." Ellen sat down in one of the wingback chairs and gazed at the gulf as Moseby jumped into her lap. "Are you ever going to tell us what has you so stressed out lately, Sue?"

"Ellen!" Tanya chastised. "She'll tell us when she's ready."

"We've been pretty patient," Ellen argued. She turned to Sue. "I wanted to ask you during the ride over, but I didn't want to distract you while you were driving."

Sue's face reddened as she crossed the room and sat beside Ellen in the adjacent wingback chair. Tanya took the chaise lounge and pulled her legs up under her, waiting for Sue to reply.

Sue wagged a finger at them. "Y'all have to promise not to discuss this with your husbands."

"These days I forget things as soon as I hear them," Ellen teased, trying to lighten the mood. "You don't have to worry about me."

Just then they heard another loud thud overhead. Again, it sounded as though something heavy had fallen onto the floor of the third story.

Tanya jumped to her feet, but before she or any of the friends could say a word, Moseby leaped from Ellen's lap and started barking at the door to the stairs.

Ellen scooped him into her arms. "What's the matter, boy?"

His bark turned into a whine, but there were other dogs barking nearby. Ellen rushed to her bedroom window and noticed the German shepherd below on his feet barking in her direction.

"What's going on, Ellen?" Tanya asked her in the bedroom doorway.

"I have no idea."

Mo leapt from her arms and barked at the stair doors again.

"Maybe we should check it out." Sue took her purse from where she'd laid it on the kitchen table and pulled out her gun. "It could be a vagrant."

Tanya gulped. "Or a demon."

Ellen scooped up her barking dog again and followed Sue up the stairs toward the third floor with Tanya close behind them.

"Wait," Tanya insisted in a whisper. "Should we call 9-1-1? What if it really is a vagrant? What if he overpowers us and hurts us?"

Sue waved her gun in the air. "That's what this is for, but maybe you're right about calling for backup. What do you think, Ellen?"

Ellen shook her head as she hugged her whining dog. "I'd hate to bother the police if it's just a raccoon up there."

Tanya took out her phone. "I'm calling Brenda, the landlord. Maybe she and her husband will come and take a look."

Ellen and Sue stood on the stairs, waiting.

"No answer," Tanya said. "It went to voicemail."

"Leave a message," Sue urged.

Tanya quickly said into her phone, "Hey, Brenda, this is Tanya Sanchez. We're in the house, but we keep hearing loud noises upstairs and are concerned there might be an animal or a vagrant. Could you and your husband please come and check it out as soon as possible?"

"I'm going up," Sue said as she continued up the stairs.

"Are you sure that's a good idea?" Tanya wondered. "Maybe we should wait for the homeowners to look into it."

"Who knows when that will be?" Sue argued. "There's no way I'm getting a wink of sleep until I know what's going on up there."

"Why don't we leave for a while?" Ellen suggested. "Let's go to the beach and give whatever's up there a chance to leave."

"That would also give Brenda time to call me back," Tanya said with a nod.

Sue hesitated on the stairs. Then another loud thud made all three friends rush down the steps and back inside the door of the second floor, closing and locking the door behind them.

Sue leaned her back against the door. "What on earth *is* that?"

"Let's hurry and get out of here," Ellen said, panting.

"To the beach, then?" Tanya asked.

"What about the pitcher of margaritas I wanted to make?" Sue reminded them. "Can we spare a few more minutes?"

Ellen cocked her head to the side. "I suppose your margaritas are worth the risk. I wanted to change into my swimwear anyway."

"Me, too," Tanya said as she headed for her room.

"Y'all get changed, and I'll have our drinks ready in no time."

Moseby stood by the door to the stairwell and growled.

CHAPTER THREE

Biloxi Beach

Directly across from their summer rental was the Biloxi Lighthouse situated on the median of Highway 90, also known as Beach Boulevard. The three friends and dog quickly descended the steps of the house and then turned left—or west—along a sidewalk toward a crosswalk. They passed an empty lot that was nothing more than a grassy hill and a few thin trees enclosed by a wrought-iron fence. A historical marker in front of it identified the location as the Robinson-Maloney-Dantzler House.

Sue stopped to read the marker aloud: "Originally a raised-cottage Greek revival mansion like Beauvoir, the house located here was built circa 1849 by J.G. Robinson, a wealthy English cotton planter. It was the center of an estate that included a ten-pin bowling alley, billiard hall, bath house, thoroughbred stables, kennels, gardens, and a wharf for docking two prized yachts. About 1908 the Maloney family enlarged the house with a second story addition and two-tiered wrap-around porches in the neo-classical style. Destroyed by Hurricane Katrina in 2005."

"How sad," Tanya said as they gazed up the hill at the empty lot.

On the other side of the lot was another white Greek revival as large as the one they were renting. A curved, stone wall surrounded by flowers near the sidewalk entrance read: *Biloxi Visitors Center.*

"Should we check it out before we get all sandy?" Ellen wondered.

Sue shook her head, her wide-brimmed hat flapping like wings. "I don't want to drink warm margaritas. Do you? This jug won't keep them cold forever."

Tanya pushed the button on the crosswalk. "There's a tour of the lighthouse in the morning at nine o'clock. Why don't we see the Visitors Center after?"

"I like that idea," Sue agreed.

When a gust of wind nearly carried her hat from her head, Ellen held onto it, slapping the top of her head while trying to keep Moseby from racing into the street. "Moseby, wait! He's anxious to see the water, I think."

They crossed the westbound traffic, stopping on the median to admire the lighthouse. The tall, white tower sat on a circular, cement foundation surrounded by a black iron fence and pretty landscaping. Although they would be touring it in the morning, Ellen walked around the structure out of curiosity, finding steps leading to the door on the east side. Near one of the gates, there was a historical marker with "1848" on it. Ellen read that this was the only active lighthouse in Mississippi to survive the devastating hurricanes of 1906, 1947, 1969, and 2005. At the top of the tower was a round observation deck.

As she stood there gazing up at the observation deck, Ellen felt like something was pressing against her chest. It was an oppressive feeling that nearly made her faint.

"Ellen?" Sue asked. "You okay?"

"I don't know . . . yes, I'll be fine. I just had a strange feeling all of a sudden."

"Me, too," Tanya admitted as she fanned herself with a magazine from her beach bag. "What do you think it means?"

"It felt like a warning," Ellen said. "I don't know. Anyway, let's get to the beach. I need a margarita."

When the light changed again, they crossed the east-bound lanes and a small parking lot where they approached a statue and another historical marker. The statue was of astronaut Fred Haise. It paid homage to his life as a fighter and research pilot and space engineer, mentioning his participation in the famous Apollo Thirteen mission.

The marker, entitled *Civil Rights Wade-Ins*, read: "On May 14, 1959, April 24, 1960, and June 23, 1963, the Biloxi beach front was the site of planned civil rights wade-ins demanding equal access to the public beach. On April 24, 1960, several citizens, both black and white, were injured and arrested, including the leader of the wade-ins, physician Dr. Gilbert R. Mason Sr. This series of protests gave birth to the Biloxi branch of the NAACP, major voter registration drives in 1960, and a 1968 federal court ruling opening the beach to all citizens."

"How interesting," Tanya remarked. "I wouldn't mind learning more about that."

"You can probably find something in the Visitors Center tomorrow," Sue pointed out. "Now let's find a place to sit before these margaritas melt."

Not far from the historical marker were a dozen sets of wooden loungers connected in pairs with an umbrella between them—some blue and others bright orange. The friends made their way to the rental hut and paid for two sets, so they could each have a chair.

Sue took a seat between Tanya and Ellen, sharing an umbrella with Tanya, and poured margaritas for each of them. Moseby sat in the empty chair beside Ellen not looking as eager to go near the water now that they were close to it. He was more interested in the gulls flying overhead.

The waves were gentle today, and, although the water was a bit murky, they sparkled in the afternoon sun. While the water was muddy, the sand was white and pristine, unlike the beaches Ellen had visited along the Texas gulf. And for a hot summer day, it wasn't very crowded. There were a few families with small children further down the beach to the west, two young men sitting in another set of rental chairs to the east, and a young man and woman holding hands as they strolled down the beach, headed east, in the direction of the Beau Rivage Casino, visible in the distance.

As Sue handed Ellen a margarita in a Styrofoam cup, Ellen said, "I'm surprised there aren't more people here."

"Well, don't jinx it," Sue said. "Let's enjoy it while we can. There may be a crowd yet."

"Where should we go for dinner tonight?" Tanya wondered as she began flipping through her magazine. "Should we try Mary Mahoney's Old French House? I heard it was good."

"It's mentioned in a book I'm reading called *Haunted Biloxi*." Sue reached into her bag and pulled out the book. "The women's restroom is supposed to be haunted. Supposedly when you look into the mirror over the sink, your reflection isn't always the thing looking back at you. I'd like to check it out."

"I thought we weren't ghost hunting on this trip," Tanya remarked.

"We're always ghost hunting," Sue said. "I'm always interested, aren't you?"

"I am," Ellen admitted. "I even brought my equipment along."

"That doesn't surprise me." Tanya smirked. "The biggest skeptic has become the biggest enthusiast."

Ellen stuck out her tongue at Tanya and then laughed.

"Do you think the noise we heard was a vagrant?" Sue asked Ellen.

"I don't know. The noises were loud. I think it was most likely a raccoon."

"Probably," Sue admitted. "But I'm hoping for a ghost. I need a new mystery to distract me."

"Not one that powerful, Sue," Tanya complained. "A ghost would have to be powerful to make that kind of noise. Please don't hope for a ghost in our rental home. Let's talk to one at Mary Mahoney's instead."

"Or better yet," Ellen began, "the cemetery. Old Biloxi Cemetery is just down the road from here. I'm hoping to capture some EVPs."

"Have you still got gas in the Pilot?" Tanya asked Sue.

"Oh, I've got gas, alright . . . fair warning," Sue said dryly. "I just don't know if it's in the Pilot."

Ellen shook her head with a laugh. "Oh, Sue." Then, after a beat, she said, "Will you tell us what's bothering you? I'm worried."

"I'm worried, too." Sue flicked a tear from the corner of one eye.

"Sue!" Tanya cried. "What's wrong?"

"I think Tom may be having an affair—if not a physical one, an emotional one, which I think is worse."

Ellen's mouth dropped open. "No way. Not Tom. What makes you think that?"

Sue took a sip of her margarita and gazed out at the gentle waves. A sailboat appeared in the distance—the only thing on the water between them and the horizon.

"He has a new assistant at work. She's not glamorous or anything, but she's fit and decent-looking and she's about our age, or maybe a little younger. Anyway, I can tell he likes her. She gave him homemade oatmeal cookies on Valentine's Day. Can you believe that? And the worst part is, he said they were the best he'd ever tasted."

"How did you find out about the cookies?" Tanya wanted to know. "If he told you about them, then I doubt there's anything going on."

"No, he didn't tell me about them. I found them when I showed up at his office one day. I'd been suspicious, so I surprised him with lunch. There they were in a tin on his desk. I said, 'What are those?' He said, 'Oatmeal cookies. They're really good—the best, in fact.' He claims that everyone in the office got some from Rhonda, but I didn't see any other tins in any of the other offices as I passed by—and believe me, I looked."

"Maybe the others took them home," Ellen pointed out. "Did you ask why he didn't?"

"He said he knew I'd eat them all."

Ellen could believe that. "But what prompted your suspicion in the first place?"

Sue sighed and took another drink. "Well, you know we sleep in separate rooms because of my snoring."

"Dave and I do, too, most nights," Tanya admitted. "I can't get used to the sound of his C-Pap machine."

"Even so, we usually have a cuddle a couple of times a month. And, as we were approaching Valentine's Day, he hadn't been to my room since Christmas. That didn't seem like him."

Ellen lowered her voice when two children ran toward the water nearby. "They say that men slow down with age. I've noticed it in Brian, too."

"He had already slowed down," Sue argued. "A couple times of month is what slowing down looks like, don't you think?"

Ellen shrugged. "Paul and I had longer droughts than that when he was alive."

"Dave and I, too. Not so much recently, but there have been droughts."

"I always know Brian's in the mood when he cooks for me," Ellen said with a grin.

Sue laughed. "You'd think I was a goddess since all I ever get from Tom are burnt offerings."

Ellen and Tanya burst out laughing.

"Wait a minute," Ellen began. "I thought Tom didn't cook."

"He doesn't, unless you count burnt toast."

Tanya tilted her head to one side. "Could something be bothering Tom, or distracting him? Maybe he hasn't been feeling well. I know with Dave, his back bothers him for weeks at a time."

"I don't think so," Sue said. "I think he's distracted by Rhonda."

"What makes you think so, other than the cookies?" Ellen asked.

"They text each other, sometimes at night while Tom and I are watching TV. You should see his face light up. It kills me."

"At night?" Tanya echoed. "That *is* suspicious."

"Tom swears it's harmless, that she's new, so she has lots of questions and often forgets to ask during business hours."

"He should put a stop to that," Ellen commented.

"He said he's told her to wait to ask during the workday, but she never does."

"Well, that's not Tom's fault," Tanya pointed out. "Maybe she has a crush on him."

"That's obvious," Sue agreed. "But he's not doing enough to discourage it."

"He's probably enjoying it," Ellen speculated. "Wouldn't you? That doesn't mean he's having an affair."

"I think he's smitten with her," Sue insisted. "I can tell he is."

"How? How can you tell?" Tanya wanted to know.

"Just the way he defends her all the time. If I say one word against her, you'd think I killed someone. His company had a retreat in March in Branson, Missouri, and he came back happier than a bee full of honey."

"That still doesn't prove anything," Ellen argued. "If he were having an affair—even an emotional one—they'd be meeting in person or talking online. A few texts in the evenings and a tin full of oatmeal cookies isn't enough to be this upset."

Tanya wrinkled her forehead. "I can't believe you're just now telling us this though. I can't believe we didn't notice how stressed you were. It took the priestess to point it out."

Sue wiped another tear from her eye. "You forget what a good actress I am."

"What does Tom think about your feelings?" Ellen asked. "Or have you masked them around him, too?"

"Well, I've told him how bothered I am. I even suggested he should fire her, but he says she's a good worker and good workers are hard to find. Oh, he's got an excuse for everything."

Tanya leaned toward Sue, putting a hand on her shoulder. "Why didn't you ask Priestess Isabel about this last night? She might have shed some light on what's going on."

Sue heaved a heavy sigh. "Because I'm afraid of the truth, and I didn't want it to spoil our trip."

"Tom is not having an affair," Ellen insisted. "He's the most loyal person I've ever met. He doesn't have it in him."

"I hope you're right," Sue said. "But I'm just not so sure you *are*."

Tanya's phone rang. "It's Brenda," she said before answering it. "Hi, Brenda . . . We're at the beach . . . What's that? . . . Really? Well, okay, great. Thanks so much."

Tanya returned her phone to her purse. "Brenda and her husband checked the third floor and didn't find anything. They said if there was an animal or a vagrant up there, it's gone now."

"Did they see any signs that anything had been disturbed?" Sue wondered.

"She didn't say. I didn't ask."

"I was wondering the same thing," Ellen murmured.

"Should I call her back?" Tanya offered.

"No, that's okay," Sue said. "But if we hear anything more, we're going up there."

Tanya drank the last of her margarita. "What if the third floor is the boundary we're not supposed to cross?"

Sue tilted her head to one side as she turned to Tanya. "Are you telling me you wouldn't be the least bit curious?"

"Of course, but . . ."

"Whatever it was is probably gone," Ellen insisted, though she sounded more confident than she felt. "I'm taking Moseby for a walk. Anyone else coming?"

CHAPTER FOUR

Mary Mahoney's Old French House

That evening, after a relaxing day at the beach, Ellen and her friends showered off and changed before heading to the restaurant. Even though they had heard no more suspicious noises in the attic, Ellen was worried about leaving Moseby, so she took him along.

Because they hadn't made reservations, or perhaps because Ellen had Moseby with her, the ladies were given a table in the courtyard, which Ellen preferred because of the vibrant garden and enormous, ancient oak tree shading the dozen tables. Vines of ivy covered the brick walls, making everything look green and lush. The shade from the tree, along with a gentle breeze, kept the hot air from stifling them. As the hostess sat them, Sue asked about the ghost in the women's bathroom.

"I've never heard that before," the young woman said with a smile. "But once a waiter here saw a shadow woman in one of the closets in the attic."

"Oh, really?" Ellen lifted her brows. "May we speak with him?"

"And would it be possible for us to visit the attic?" Sue asked.

"I'll have to ask the owner," the hostess said as she handed over the menus. "Your waiter will be right with you."

A little bit later, after their waiter took their order, he brought over the young man who'd seen the figure in the attic.

"It was a woman in an old-timey dress," the young man said. "She looked like the same woman in the painting that's stored in that same closet."

Ellen wrinkled her brow. "How strange."

"Where is this painting?" Sue asked.

"In a closet in the attic," the young man said again.

Ellen leaned forward. "May we see it?"

"Here comes the owner," their waiter said. "You can ask him."

A tall, robust man with a bald head and bright smile approached their table. He reminded Ellen of Mr. Clean. "Good evening, ladies. I was told I needed to come talk to you. What do you want to know? The house was built in 1737 by a Frenchman who moved here after the fall of Napoleon. He built two houses—exact replicas—one here and another in New Orleans. We acquired it in 1962 and opened it as a restaurant in 1964—my mother, Mary, and her brother, Andrew Cvitanovich. They were Croatian. She spoke fluent Croatian. We had a Cajun chef, an African American chef, and an Italian maître d'. We were in a French house. My dad was Irish. We had African American waiters."

"Quite an international ensemble," Ellen quickly said, trying to get a word in edgewise.

"That's exactly what my mother used to say. But everybody's Irish on St. Patrick's Day," he continued, "and my mother, along with the O'Keefes, started the Hibernian Society in the early seventies, and that's when they had the first big parades on St. Patrick's Day. She was a wonderful woman, my mother, working in what they called a man's world. She used to feel bad that she didn't have a talent. Her brother could paint, and her father could play piano. But Father Mullen, her mentor, used to say that her talent was people. And it was true. Mother had a talent with people. I like to say she had a degree in social engineering. Oh, look up there at that Cardinal. See it?"

He pointed to the balcony above where a red bird perched on the rail.

"Your mother's come to hear what you have to say about her," Sue teased.

"She knows what I have to say about her. She knows I adore her. Everyone who knew her did. They couldn't help it. They say you haven't really visited Biloxi if you haven't eaten at Mary Mahoney's. In 1984, she fed the president on the lawn of the White House. We've fed presidents, diplomats, celebrities, and ordinary people this same good food for over fifty years. Hurricane Katrina tried to take this place down—and me right along with it—in 2005, but after eight weeks, we were one of the first places to open our doors. We opened with the same menu we closed with."

"Do you feel a lot of competition from the casinos?" Sue asked.

"We love the casinos. They bring in more tourists. Just like the manmade beach with its white sand up and down the gulf. It was all to build up tourism. The casinos play their part, and so do we. Did you ladies know that when we voted in Harrison County in the early nineties to legalize gambling that Biloxi voted in favor by seventy percent? And D'Iberville was about the same. But Gulfport voted against it forty-five to fifty-five percent, and Long Beach voted against it thirty-five to sixty-five. City of Pass Christian? Fifty-fifty. You know why? You know what Biloxi has that they don't have? We have seven of them in Biloxi. They have two of them in Gulfport."

"What?" Ellen asked, taking the bait.

"Catholic churches." Bob chuckled and slapped his thigh. "When you told a Catholic about gambling, he didn't say, 'Oh, no,' he said, 'Where at?' And you know, we got the French, Croatian, and Irish, and they're all Catholic."

Ellen and her friends chuckled.

"It's refreshing, isn't it?" Sue asked her friends.

"What is?" Bob wanted to know.

"To meet a man who isn't a man of few words," Sue said with a laugh.

"Did you know that women say on average 30,000 words a day and men say only 15,000? Women talk twice as much as men. It's a fact. That's what a wife told her husband. He said, 'Why is that, hun?' She said, 'Because we women have to repeat everything to you men.' After she got done telling him this, you know what he said?"

"What?" Ellen asked.

Bob grinned. "'What did you say, hun?'"

Ellen shook her head. "Boo, Mr. Mahoney!"

"I guess you didn't like that one. But listen to this. Did you know that the older we get, the more valuable we become?"

Sue smirked. "Tell that to my husband."

"We get silver in our hair, gold in our teeth, natural stones in our kidneys, gas in our stomachs, and lead in our feet."

The three friends exchanged grins.

Ellen threw her head back. "You made up with that last one, Mr. Mahoney."

"Call me Bob. Mr. Mahoney was my father."

"Now, tell us if this restaurant is haunted, Bob," Sue said, getting to the point. "One of your waiters mentioned seeing the woman from one of the paintings in the attic. May we see it?"

"I've not heard that. Our resident ghost is called Angelique—Angelique Fayard."

"Oh?" Tanya asked. "Do you know anything about her?"

"Not really, except that she was one of the first European settlers to own land in Biloxi. I've never seen or spoken to her. I've just heard stories about her from my mother, my uncle, and some of our staff."

"What do they say?" Ellen asked.

"She likes to walk around and say what's what. But no one ever hangs around long enough to listen. Sometimes she appears as a shadow and other times as a woman in white."

Ellen and her friends exchanged looks. Ellen wondered how Bob would feel about allowing them to do a paranormal investigation in the attic.

"Excuse me ladies," he said suddenly. "One of my employees is flagging me down."

The owner left their table before Ellen could ask her question.

After a delicious meal of fish stuffed with crabmeat and a rich cream sauce over pasta—the most delectable entrée Ellen had ever eaten—Ellen leaned forward, cradling Moseby in his cloth pooch carrier, and said just above a whisper, "I'm going to look for the attic. Would either of you like to come with me?"

"Bob didn't agree to that, did he?' Tanya asked.

Ellen shrugged. "Not exactly, but he didn't say it was off limits, either. What could it hurt? If I'm not allowed up there, well, at least I tried."

Sue turned to Tanya. "We can't all go, or they'll think we walked out on our bill."

"I'll stay and take care of the check," Tanya offered. "You two go ahead."

"Are you sure?" Ellen asked, not wanting to leave Tanya out.

"I'm sure."

Ellen led the way through the courtyard and back to the main entrance of the restaurant with Sue on her heels. Inside near the bar, she asked a passing waiter, "Can you direct me to the attic?"

"Straight up those steps and to your left," the waiter replied before leaving the bar with a tray of drinks.

Ellen glanced back at Sue, who grinned mischievously.

"Lead the way," Sue sang.

Ellen followed the waiter's directions and found another longer, steeper set of stairs leading to the left, to what she supposed was the attic. Although there were buffet tables dressed in linens and set with tableware, the room was dark except for the light from the sunset washing in from the windows.

Ellen rummaged through her purse. "I have my EVP recorder, spirit box, pendulum, and EMF detector. Ready to investigate?"

"I am if you are. If someone comes up, we'll just say Bob said it was okay, and then, before they can discover otherwise, we'll make a run for it."

"I like the way you think."

Sue glanced around. "There are four doors up here, Ellen. Are they all closets? You try those two and I'll try these."

A fireplace separated the two sets of doors, and although there was a painting over it, it was not of a woman but of the sea—the gulf, Ellen thought.

She opened the first door, using the light on her phone to see by. "Nothing in this one. Just some electrical wires and duct work."

"Same over here."

Ellen tried the second door. "This one's either stuck or locked."

"Over here, Ellen. I think this is it."

Ellen rushed to Sue's side and peered into the closet. A portrait of a woman standing on a staircase in a Victorian dress peered back at her.

Ellen quickly snapped a photo. "Maybe we can find out who she is."

"Give me your EMF detector."

Sue took a few readings while Ellen turned on her EVP recorder and asked, "Is there anyone here with us? Any spirits from the other realm? We mean no harm. We only wish to talk with you."

"Do you feel that?" Sue asked.

"I've got chills."

"It got cold fast."

"Is anyone here with us?" Ellen asked again just as the EMF detector spiked. "We might not be able to hear you now, but later, when we listen back to this recorder, we may be able to. If you have something to say, we're here to listen."

There was a creak in the attic behind them. Ellen and Sue turned.

"I think someone's coming," Sue whispered. "Quick, hide."

The two friends tip-toed inside the closet and closed the door behind them. They turned off their light in case it might be seen beneath the door. Moseby whined.

Ellen stroked his curly hair. "Sshh."

It was creepy in the small closet in the dark with the strange chill that had crept up on them. Ellen could hear Sue breathing beside her, along with the sound of her own heart pounding in her chest. Moseby continued to whine.

"Quiet, boy," Ellen said softly.

She was startled by the feeling of a hand on her shoulder. For a moment, she couldn't speak.

"Sue?" Ellen finally whispered. "Are you touching me?"

"Sorry. My legs are cramping."

Ellen sighed with relief but then froze again when she heard footsteps right outside the closet door. She held her breath and heard Sue doing the same. They waited for several seconds. All the while, Ellen prayed that Moseby would be a good boy.

After a minute or two had passed, she let out the breath she'd been holding and attempted to open the door.

"Oh, no," she said. "It won't open."

"What?" Sue turned on her phone light and rattled the knob. "We're trapped in here? Oh, God."

Moseby whined again.

"I'm calling Tanya," Ellen said.

But before she could call her friend for help, the attic door swung open, and a bright light was thrust into their eyes.

"Ellen? Sue?"

It was Tanya.

The two friends laughed hysterically as they stepped from the closet. Ellen was so relieved that her eyes welled with tears.

"You scared the living daylights out of me," Sue complained.

"Sorry," Tanya said. "It seemed like you guys had been gone a while. Thought I'd come and check on you."

Ellen showed Tanya the painting. "We think that's the woman the waiter saw. It's the only painting of a woman in an old-timey dress up here. I snapped a photo. Maybe we can find out who she is."

"Feel how cold it is in there," Sue insisted.

Tanya stepped inside. "It really is cold. I've got goosebumps—look." She held out her arm. The hair on her forearm stood on end. "I feel anxious in here, too."

"Let's try the pendulum," Ellen suggested as she dug for it in her purse. "Hold on, Moseby-Mo. Just a few more minutes."

Ellen held the pendulum over an open palm, trying to hold still. "My hands are shaking too much."

"Let me try." Sue took the long chain in one hand and stopped the pyramid-shaped pendant from moving with the other. "Is there someone here with us who would like to talk to us? If so, please move this pendulum in a circular motion. If you want us to leave, move it back and forth, like this." Sue quickly demonstrated and then stopped the pendulum again.

The three friends watched on as the pendulum began to move, swinging in a circular motion.

"They have a message," Tanya said.

"It's too bad we don't have the Ouija Board with us," Ellen mumbled.

"What if we make one?" Sue suggested. "I have some paper and a pen in my purse."

"Make one? How?" Tanya wanted to know.

She and Ellen watched on as Sue wrote the alphabet out in a clockwise circle on a piece of paper. Then she wrote "YES" on one end of the page and "NO" on the other. "I'll hold the pendulum over the paper."

Ellen lifted her brows. "What a great idea."

"I've been known to have a few."

"Here." Tanya held her hands out, palms up, like a table. "Put the paper here."

Sue did as Tanya said and then dangled the pendulum over the paper. "Spirit of the other realm, we want to hear your message. Please swing this pendulum along one letter in the alphabet at a time, so we can spell out what you have to say."

After a few seconds, the pendulum began to swing back and forth from the L to the Z.

"Ellen, write down L slash Z," Sue instructed. Ellen took the pen Sue had used and scrounged through her purse for something to write on. She found an old receipt and wrote L/Z.

"It shifted," Tanya pointed out. "I think it's D and O."

Ellen wrote D/O.

"Now it's G and S," Sue said. "Does that spell anything yet? Maybe this is working."

Ellen wrote G/S. "Zog or log. I don't know. Keep trying."

"H and T," Tanya said.

Ellen wrote it down.

"A and M," Sue said. "Is there a pattern yet?"

"Just keep going," Ellen said. "We'll look for a pattern after it stops."

"D and O again, I think," Tanya said.

"Yes," Sue agreed. "That's right."

Ellen recorded the D/O.

"Now it's shifted to C and N, hasn't it?" Tanya asked. "Or was that you, Sue?"

"I'm holding it was still as I can. Just write it down, just in case."

Ellen did as she said.

"It scooted just a bit to E and P," Tanya observed. "I don't know if this is working. It's barely shifting over."

"Let's just keep going," Ellen said again. "Now what's it on?"

"K and Y," Sue replied. "Is that what you're seeing Tanya?"

"Yes."

Just then, as if grabbed by another hand, the pendulum stopped.

Ellen's mouth gaped. "Did you do that, Sue?"

"I don't think so."

"I hear someone coming," Tanya said. "Maybe we should go."

Suddenly, the lights overhead came on, and a young woman gasped at the sight of them.

"Goodness," the young woman carrying a tray said. "You scared me."

"Bob said we could come up here," Sue quickly said. "We're paranormal investigators."

"Oh, that's what's going on," the waitress said. "My manager thought it was raccoons again."

"No, just us," Tanya said. "But we're leaving now. Please thank Mr. Mahoney for us."

"Or better yet," Sue said, following Tanya and Ellen to the stairs, "don't say anything at all."

The three friends scurried from the restaurant and to the Honda Pilot as fast as their legs could carry them.

CHAPTER FIVE

Mixed Messages

Once they were in the car, first Ellen, and then Tanya, tried to make sense of the letters Ellen had recorded on the back of an old receipt during their session in the attic of Mary Mahoney's Old French House.

"I see 'ghost Monday,'" Tanya said. "Does that mean anything?"

"Give me that." Sue reached for the receipt from behind the wheel and studied it. "I can't make heads or tails of it either. Maybe we weren't talking to a ghost after all."

"Let's go to the Beau Rivage and forget about it for a while," Tanya suggested. "I feel a winning streak coming on. And maybe a fresh perspective will help us see the ghost's message later."

Since the casino wasn't far from the Mary Mahoney parking lot, the ladies decided to leave the car and walk. Ellen leashed Mo before she and her friends made their way down and across the street and up through the manicured and lush landscape of the hotel. Once they reached the beautiful fountain and signage, she tucked Mo back into his carrier, holding him like a mother would a newborn baby. Ready to claim he was her emotional support animal if needed, she was relieved when no one stopped her from bringing him into the establishment.

With the issue of her dog settled, Ellen glanced around the grand entrance in awe. It was an atrium with trees, shrubs, and flowers—as pretty as those on the outside—growing on the inside, separated from the cream, blue, and orange floral carpet by nothing but short and curvy stone edging. Bright orange and purple lights in the shape of butterflies sparkled in some of the trees, reaching up to high ceilings where enormous, ornamental chandeliers created focal points throughout the luxurious space, as did skylights so large that they reminded Ellen of *Willy Wonka and the Chocolate Factory*.

Everywhere she looked, there were shops, restaurants, and bars trimmed with cream-colored crown moldings, awnings, corbels, and sconces. As large as any mall, the hotel casino was more than Ellen had expected to encounter in a small Mississippi coastal town.

"Let's hit the slots!" Tanya cried enthusiastically as they made their way through the lobby toward the casino.

Two guards asked for an ID but once again did not bat an eye at Ellen's precious cargo. A couple dressed in fancy clothes entered behind them. They appeared to be the same age as Ellen and her friends, but the woman was a looker, her body perfectly toned without an ounce of loose arm or neck fat.

When the couple was out of earshot, Ellen whispered, "I wish I knew the secret to a smoking hot body at our age."

"That's easy," Sue said. "Cremation."

Ellen giggled.

"Or plastic surgery," Tanya said. "I'm thinking of looking into it."

Ellen rolled her eyes. "You don't need surgery, Tanya—not that there's anything wrong with it. What am I saying? You go, girl. If you want surgery, go for it."

"I'm just thinking about it. Now, where should we start?"

"You two go ahead," Ellen said. "I'm going to see if I can make anything out of this message."

"But we have all week to do that," Sue argued. "Don't you want to have some fun?"

"This *is* fun," she insisted.

She watched Sue and Tanya head for the slot machines, wondering if she should force herself to join them, but her curiosity over the ghostly message won out, and she turned with Mo to find a place to sit down. Off in one corner near a bar where a widescreen television was playing a music video, Ellen sat on a big and comfy, tan, leather sofa and pulled out her phone and the old receipt where she had scribbled the enigmatic message.

When she had no luck attempting to decode the letters, she decided to Google "Angelique Fayard," but not much turned up in her search results except for a short article confirming that Angelique and her husband, Jean Baptiste Fayard, were granted 500 acres of land in 1784 on the Biloxi peninsula from the gulf to the Back Bay, bounded on the west by Porter Ave. and on the east by Lameuse St.

Ellen opened Google Maps to find that the tract of land encompassed everything from the Hard Rock Café, including Mary

Mahoney's Old French House, all the way west past the Biloxi Lighthouse.

"This was once her land," Ellen muttered.

Moseby looked up at her and licked her chin.

"Yes, boy. I'm onto something."

She opened the photo gallery on her phone to study the photo she took of the painting in the attic. She flinched in her seat at the surprising appearance of a shadowy figure standing beside the painting. It clearly wasn't her own shadow, because the flash had been on her phone in front of her. And it wasn't Sue's either. She had been standing behind her. Ellen could think of nothing that could have cast that shadow.

Had she captured the ghost of Angelique Fayard?

Moseby squirmed in his carrier.

"You need to go outside, Moseby-Mo?"

He licked her chin again.

"Okay. Let's go."

She texted Sue and Tanya that she was going for a walk, and then she left the casino, returning to Beach Boulevard, where she leashed Mo and let him walk on the sidewalk. He sniffed at the pretty landscaping and then continued to the east, in the direction of Mary Mahoney's.

As they walked in the warm night air, made bright by streetlights and the blinking signs along the strip, Ellen continued to mull over what she'd discovered about Angelique. Though it wasn't much, it gave her some context. A woman who had once owned this entire tract of land was trying to tell her something. Perhaps she'd been trying to relay this same message for centuries, but no one had been able to understand it.

Ellen returned from her reverie as she and Mo were passing the Hard Rock Café and were now stopped at a traffic light on, of all streets, Lameuse St. This would have been the eastern border of Angelique's property. When the light changed, she and Mo walked across Beach Boulevard toward a park. Moseby seemed happy to have grass beneath his paws and trees overhead. Feeling bad that he hadn't had time to run around, she let him take the lead through the park, sniffing and prancing to his heart's content.

Soon they came upon a memorial that Ellen remembered reading about years ago—a memorial to those lives lost on the Mississippi gulf coast to Hurricane Katrina. It was a twelve-foot wall with a tile mosaic of a wave on one end and the names etched in black granite on the other. There was also a glass case containing rubble from the destruction.

Ellen sat on a stone bench across from the memorial to have a rest. Mo sat on the ground beside her, panting.

"I need to get you out more," she said to him. "You're in about as good of shape as I am."

As she gazed at the memorial across from her, she said a little prayer for the victims.

Her prayer was interrupted by a text from Sue, asking her where she was.

"Tanya has lost $500," Sue wrote.

"So much for Isabel's predictions," Ellen wrote back. "I'm on my way. Be there in fifteen."

Ellen met up with her friends in the hotel lobby.

"Maybe she was wrong," Tanya said with a shrug. "Maybe she was wrong about everything."

"We all have our good days and our bad days," Ellen conceded. "At least you stopped when you did."

Sue put her hands on her hips. "Ain't that the truth. I thought I was going to have to call in the armed forces to help me pull her away from those machines."

"I was so sure I was going to hit the jackpot."

"Well, in a way, we did hit the jackpot," Ellen said, taking out her phone. She pulled up the photo of the painting in the attic. "Take a look at this and tell me what you see."

"Is that a shadow woman?" Sue asked.

"I think it's Angelique Fayard. Let me tell you what I've learned about her."

As they headed back to the car at Mary Mahoney's, Ellen relayed the little bit of information she had found on their mysterious ghost woman.

"I wonder if she lived at Mary Mahoney's Old French House," Tanya wondered.

Ellen nodded. "That's what I was thinking."

"There's bound to be a record somewhere that can confirm that," Sue pointed out as they reached their car.

Back at their rental house, Ellen and her friends changed into their pajamas, and Ellen fed Mo, before getting comfortable in the living room. It was too hot to sit on the balcony and too dark to see the ocean, for the sky was overcast tonight, but a golden beam shot across the sea from the lighthouse, blinking in threes every few minutes, creating a gorgeous light show in the dark clouds. Ellen could only imagine what a comfort that light had been to sailors returning home to the gulf coast over the decades.

Sitting in one of the wingback chairs with Sue in the other, Ellen put a hand on her friend's arm. "You doing okay?"

"As well as can be expected, I suppose."

"Have you spoken to Tom?"

Sue grinned.

"What's so funny?" Tanya asked from the chaise lounge.

"Men are so easy to scare," Sue replied.

Ellen covered her mouth. "Oh, no. What did you do?"

Sue's smile widened. "I asked Tom if he knew what today was. After thirty years of marriage, that still gets him frazzled—every single time."

Tanya chuckled. "Oh, Sue."

"Way to keep him on his toes," Ellen said admiringly.

"He says he's at home alone watching television," Sue said. "And I'm choosing to believe him."

"You should," Ellen insisted.

"Oh, that's him calling," Sue said.

As Sue left the room answering her phone, Ellen revisited the letter sequence on the back of her old receipt: L/Z, D/O, G/S, H/T, A/M, D/O, C/N, E/P, K/Y.

A thud overhead made her look up from the receipt.

"Not again," Tanya groaned.

"That wasn't thunder, was it?" Ellen said, though she really didn't think it was.

Tanya shook her head.

Sue re-entered the room. "Do you think something, or someone, left and came back?" She took out her gun and told Tom that the noises had returned.

"Could it just be the pipes or the air conditioner?" Ellen wondered. "Maybe that's a regular house noise."

Sue put one hand on her hip. "Come on, Ellen. You know that's not normal."

"Take it easy with that gun," Ellen said.

"I'm just going to go up there and knock on the door," Sue said. "Maybe I'll scare whatever is up there away." Then, into the phone, she said, "I promise I'm being careful."

"Are you sure that's a good idea?" Tanya jumped to her feet, too. "Maybe we should call the homeowners—or better yet, the police."

"I'm okay with that," Sue said. "Call 9-1-1."

Shaking a little, Ellen took out her phone. "Here I go."

It took only a few seconds for someone to answer on the other end. "Nine-one-one, what's your emergency?"

"Hello, I'm staying in a summer rental on Beach Boulevard, and I think there might be an intruder on the top floor."

"Address please?"

Ellen covered the phone. "Tanya? What's the address?"

Sue piped up, "Ten twenty-two Beach Boulevard."

Ellen repeated the address to the 9-1-1 operator.

"I'll get someone there as soon as I can. Hold the line for just a moment."

"They're sending someone out," Ellen said to her friends as adrenaline pumped through her.

"Thank you for holding, who am I speaking to?"

"This is Ellen Mohr—er, McManius. Sorry. Mohr was my name, but I remarried after my first husband died."

"Tell me why you suspect there's an intruder."

Ellen told the operator about the thuds hitting the floor, how they asked the homeowners to check on things while they were at the beach, and how the noise had returned tonight.

"It might just be an animal," Ellen admitted, "but we're rather terrified it might not be."

"Have you tried contacting the homeowners again tonight?"

"No, ma'am. Should we?"

"It would be helpful. Unless we have reasonable cause, we won't be able to enter a locked unit."

Ellen covered the phone and asked Tanya to call Brenda, explaining what the operator had said. Before she'd finished explaining, she heard sirens.

"Are those sirens for us?" Ellen asked the operator.

"Yes, ma'am, but don't hang up with me until we have an officer in the room with you."

Ellen heard footsteps coming up the stairs. Sue put her gun away and opened the door to the stairwell. Two officers entered.

"They're here," Ellen said into the phone. "Thanks for everything."

"Good luck, Mrs. McManius."

Sue was already telling the two officers—one male and the other female—about the noises they'd been hearing upstairs. Ellen scooped up Moseby to keep him quiet.

"The homeowners aren't answering their phone," Tanya said.

"You ladies stay down here," the female officer—a tall brunette—said. "We'll go up and have a look."

"I'll call you back, Tom," Sue said into her phone.

The officers were gone for ten minutes—which had seemed much longer to Ellen.

"The door's locked, and there's a sign on the door that says 'Danger. Under construction. Do not enter,'" the male officer, who was short and round, explained. "Any luck getting ahold of the homeowners?"

"No," Tanya said. "I've tried calling and texting."

"Everything's quiet up there right now," the woman said. "If you'd like, we can stay for a few minutes, to see if the noises return."

"That would be great," Sue said.

"Can I make you some tea?" Tanya offered.

"Thank you, ma'am," the man said. "That would be nice."

The officers stayed for twenty minutes, and during that time, the thud from upstairs did not repeat itself. Tanya tried several more times to call the homeowners but got no answer.

"If you hear something again," the woman said, "don't hesitate to call us. That's what we're here for."

"Thank you," Sue said as the officers left.

Alone again, Ellen let Moseby down from her arms as she collapsed in a chair. "What a riot."

"It was probably nothing," Tanya began, "but better safe than sorry, I guess."

"They were pretty nice about not making us feel as though we'd wasted their time," Sue put in.

Tanya yawned. "I guess I'll turn in. Are you guys staying up?"

"Not too much longer," Ellen said. "I want to work on this message some more." She waved the old receipt with the ghost letters on the back.

"I think I'll have a few crackers, and then I'll hit it, too," Sue said.

Tanya crossed the living room toward her room. "Good night then."

"Good night," Ellen and Sue said together.

Ellen focused once more on the letter sequence: L/Z, D/O, G/S, H/T, A/M, D/O, C/N, E/P, K/Y.

"Oh, my gosh! It's plain as day!" Ellen leapt to her feet to show Sue and Tanya. Moseby danced around her legs excitedly. "Lost money! It says lost money!"

CHAPTER SIX

Biloxi Lighthouse

Ellen and Moseby followed Tanya and Sue down the sidewalk and across the street to the Biloxi Lighthouse early Friday morning for their nine o'clock tour. A tall, thin woman in her early seventies was waiting just outside the circular gate on the eastern side. A young couple and an older gentleman were already there waiting, too, as Ellen and her friends approached.

"Good morning and welcome," the woman at the gate greeted. "If you want to climb up, you'll need a bracelet. You can get one for five dollars from the Visitors Center."

Ellen and her friends didn't have bracelets.

"I'll run over and get some for us," Tanya offered. "I'll be right back."

"Why don't you go after I give you a bit of history?" the guide suggested.

"Will there be enough time?" Tanya asked.

"Yes. I'll just speak for a few minutes, and then the rest of your tour is self-guided."

Tanya nodded. "Sounds good."

"Please come close, so you can hear my voice over the sounds of morning traffic."

As Ellen moved closer to the lighthouse, she felt the same oppressive feeling she'd had the day before while standing near it. It was an anxious feeling, like someone was trying to warn her about something.

Without asking for their names or hometowns, the guide launched into a monologue about the lighthouse. "It's one of the oldest surviving, active lighthouses on the entire gulf coast. It's served as a beacon to travelers by both air and sea for over one hundred and fifty years. It has survived the devastation of over a dozen major hurricanes, and although construction and progress has changed much about Biloxi, this lighthouse has remained a constant. Every night, without fail, it lights up the night with its flashing signal that means welcome to Biloxi."

The tour guide opened the gate and invited everyone to step inside, where they paused near the exterior door to the building.

"At sixty-five feet tall from its base to the tip of the weathervane and nearly fifteen feet wide at its base, this cast-iron lighthouse, designed by a company called Murray and Hazlehurst, was built in 1848 for what was once the most prominent harbor for the busiest port on the gulf—New Orleans. Nothing has changed about this structure except the light. It became electric in the 1920s and automated in 1939. At one time, the lighthouse was painted black with tar as a waterproofing agent, but after boat captains complained that they couldn't see it because of the trees in the background, it was painted white again. There used to be a keeper's building where the lighthouse keepers dwelled but, unlike the structure behind me, it did not survive."

The guide unlocked and opened the lighthouse door.

"The building was carefully engineered with a series of connecting cast-iron plates on the outside and a layer of brick on the inside. At the time of its construction, only one other lighthouse of its kind had been built in America. Some people thought the plan to use this relatively new material to be risky."

"I guess they thought wrong," Sue said with a grin.

"Indeed," the guide said with a nod. "Construction of the lighthouse and the adjacent building for its keeper was completed in six weeks. Only six people have held the title of keeper, three of which were women, and those women maintained the light for 74 of the light's 91 years of human service."

"That's interesting," the older man said.

"Indeed," the guide said again. "Imagine being a widow with small children and having to climb all fifty-seven steps to the top every few hours in the heat or in the dark of night, especially during a storm. And if it was a hurricane, the keeper's job was to weather the storm at the top, waiting for the destruction to end before coming down again."

"Fifty-seven steps?" Sue echoed. "I think I'll wait for you down here."

"It's a vigorous climb, to be sure," the guide said. "And to reach the top, you must climb an eight-rung ladder through the trapdoor. Those with bracelets are welcome to get started. Please note the watermarks from various storm surges over the years along your way up. I'll be waiting for you down here but must lock up at ten, so be sure to come out by then, or you'll be trapped here until tomorrow morning." The guide didn't even crack a smile.

"Be right back," Tanya said.

"Don't get one for me," Sue reminded her.

"Or me," Ellen said.

Tanya frowned. "What? Don't you want to go up?"

Ellen sighed. "Fifty-seven steps? It looks a lot further up from inside than it did on the outside."

"But imagine the view," Tanya prodded.

"Why don't we walk with her to the Visitors Center?" Sue suggested to Ellen. "We can look around instead of waiting for her down here."

Ellen turned to the guide. "By any chance, do you know anything about an Angelique Fayard?"

"I've heard of the name but that's the extent of my knowledge."

"What about lost money?" Sue asked. "Are there any legends about old French coins shipwrecked nearby, or anything like that?"

"None that I'm aware of."

They thanked their guide and headed back across the street, where they followed a path up the hill to the house. Eleven steps made of red pavers welcomed them to a wrap-around porch. Ellen put Moseby into his cloth pooch carrier as she followed Tanya and Sue into a spacious foyer with high tray ceilings flanked by two large parlors, each with a fireplace and bright, floor-to-ceiling windows. In the center of the foyer, they found a stand with a guest book.

"I guess I'll skip the climb up the lighthouse, too," Tanya said.

Ellen put a hand on her friend's shoulder. "I don't want you to miss out. I'll go with you if it's important to you."

"No, that's okay."

"I'll sign the guestbook for us," Sue offered.

To the right of the guestbook was a large reception desk and to the left were elaborately beaded gowns. Beyond the gowns were displays about Biloxi's history from the time of its first French settlers in 1699 to present day.

Ellen was drawn past the reception desk to a long corridor with a wall of informational pamphlets about things to do in Biloxi. That's when she saw the gift shop and the little lighthouse ornaments. She had to buy one. She'd been collecting Christmas ornaments from her travels for years now, and a lighthouse ornament from Biloxi would make the perfect addition to her growing collection.

From the gift shop, they toured a museum at the back of the house and then climbed a lovely winding staircase to the second floor, where they watched a fifteen-minute movie about the history of Biloxi and its diverse culture before making their way downstairs again.

As they were descending, Tanya pointed to a window. "I read that six stained-glass windows were salvaged from the Dantzler House after Hurricane Katrina. At the time it was destroyed, the house was owned by the city and was used for office space and such. Apparently, the Dantzler House provided a footprint for this house, which was built in 2016."

"So, it isn't historical?" Ellen was surprised. "I thought it had been refurbished."

"The house we're staying at is one of the few truly refurbished historical homes left on the Biloxi coast," Tanya explained.

Before leaving, Ellen tracked down one of the docents from the museum and asked about Angelique Fayard, but the woman's answer was no different from that of their lighthouse guide—the name was familiar but nothing more. Ellen also asked about legends of lost money in Biloxi, maybe old French money lost at sea, but again the docent shrugged.

Ellen tucked the pamphlets she'd collected into her bag as she and her friends made their way through the foyer and back out to the porch, where Moseby was glad to be freed from his carrier. Then she followed her friends down the steps and back toward their summer rental.

"McElroy's Harbor House for lunch?" Sue asked as they walked along the sidewalk against the flow of traffic on Beach Boulevard.

"Sounds good to me," Tanya said.

"Let's do it," Ellen agreed.

When they reached the house, the German shepherd on the lawn of the house behind theirs lifted his head and then laid it back down again. Ellen wondered if he was ever walked or let inside. What a sad existence to be chained to a stake.

She and her friends decided to pile into the Pilot and go directly to McElroy's, which was only a short drive away, just past the Hard Rock Café. They took an elevator up to the restaurant overlooking the harbor, where vessels of varying sizes were docked. Ellen was relieved that nobody stopped her from bringing Moseby inside because she didn't want to leave him in the hot car, even with the window cracked open.

They were seated beside a window with panoramic views of the gulf.

"How beautiful," Tanya said. "Can you imagine looking out at this every day?"

"I'd move to the coast in a heartbeat if it weren't for the threat of hurricanes." Sue admitted.

Ellen nodded. "I suppose everything in life is a compromise of some kind."

After the waitress had taken their orders, Sue leaned over the table. "So, when are we going back to Mary Mahoney's to talk to Angelique again?"

Ellen raised a brow. "I was wondering the same thing. Should we go there tonight?"

"I could certainly eat there again," Tanya said. "The food was delicious. Should we try to get reservations this time, so we can eat inside?"

Ellen shrugged. "I really enjoyed the courtyard, but I suppose it wouldn't hurt, just in case."

"I'll call them now." Sue pulled out her phone.

Ellen left the table for a few minutes to use the restroom. At the sink, Moseby drank some water from her hand.

"You've been such a good boy. I'm so lucky Brian found you."

Back at the table, Sue had bad news. Mary Mahoney's was completely booked, and a table was unlikely to become available on a Friday night.

"But I was able to get us reservations for Sunday evening," Sue explained.

"What if we play slots next door at the Hard Rock Café and take food home with us to eat later tonight?" Tanya suggested. "I'm eager to win all that money the priestess predicted I would win."

"You said yourself, she could have been wrong," Ellen pointed out. "But since I didn't play any last night, I'm game to go today. Sue? What do you think?"

"Let's do it."

It was dusk by the time they left the Hard Rock Café and Casino with to-go boxes of burgers and fries. Ellen fed Moseby a few of her fries in the back seat of the Pilot as Sue drove them west on Beach Boulevard. As they neared their summer rental, Ellen was once again amazed by what a powerful beacon the lighthouse served on the Mississippi gulf coast.

"I'm regretting my decision not to climb up to the top of the lighthouse today," she admitted to her friends. "Tanya, you were right. The view must be spectacular."

"We have all week," Tanya pointed out. "We can go any day you want."

"Is there someone up there *now*?" Sue asked. "I see someone—a woman, I think—standing up there on the observation deck."

Ellen squinted. "I don't see anyone."

"Me, neither."

"I know I'm not crazy." Sue passed their rental home to get closer to the lighthouse.

"That makes one of us," Ellen teased.

Sue pulled into the parking lot near Biloxi Beach and the Point Cadet sign. "Are you telling me you don't see a woman up there?"

Ellen squinted again. "Sue, I honestly don't."

"Wait," Tanya said, "I saw a shadow move up there. I can't tell if it's a person, though."

Sue continued to gaze up through the windshield toward the top of the tower. "I don't see her anymore."

Moseby began to whine. Then, the door to the lighthouse, which was supposed to be locked, swung open.

"What the heck?" Sue cried.

The three friends waited, holding their breaths, but no one emerged.

Sue cut the engine. "I'm going to check it out. Anyone coming?"

"I won't have you going alone," Tanya said.

Ellen climbed from the back seat with Mo. "The guide did say it was kept locked at all times, didn't she?"

"She made a point of it," Sue reminded her. "She said we would be locked inside until the next morning if we didn't leave by ten."

They crossed the street to the median and approached the black gate. The door to the lighthouse swung back and forth in the wind.

"Hello?" Sue shouted with her hand hidden in her purse—probably fingering her gun. "Is somebody in there?"

Moseby whined on his leash and moved between Ellen's legs. Ellen scooped him up. "It's okay, boy."

Tanya flipped on the flashlight on her phone and shined it inside. "I don't see anyone."

Sue turned to Ellen. "You were just saying you wanted to go up. Here's your chance."

"There could be a killer up there!" Tanya objected.

"Wait, what's that?" Sue pointed across the street, toward the Visitors Center. "Do y'all see her?"

Ellen sucked in air at the sight of a shadow woman standing on the corner across the street from them. Wearing a Victorian-style dress, she looked exactly like the shadow Ellen had caught in her photo of the attic closet at Mary Mahoney's.

"Angelique Fayard?" Ellen whispered.

Moseby whined again.

"It's okay, boy," Ellen said, setting him down on his feet.

The shadow woman beckoned.

"I see her," Tanya said. "Should we follow her?"

"Of course, we should," Sue insisted. "Come on."

When the light turned, they crossed the street, only to find that the shadow woman had vanished.

Sue pointed west, in the direction away from their summer rental. "There she is. See her?"

Ellen had lost sight of her, but she trusted her friend. "Follow her. Come on."

They crossed Porter Avenue—the western border of what was once Angelique Fayard's land—and a tree-lined park before Ellen saw her again standing on the next corner. Every time the ladies caught up to her, the apparition disappeared only to reappear a block away. Eventually, they found themselves at the Old Biloxi Cemetery.

"There she is!" Sue, panting now, said as she pointed a finger.

The shadow woman was bent over a memorial stone obelisk. The three friends headed down a winding gravel road toward her, and once again, as they neared her, she vanished. They glanced around, hoping she would appear to them again, but after several minutes, they gave up.

"Maybe she led us to this headstone for a reason," Tanya said as she bent over the obelisk to read it. "Peter Halat, Sr., 1915-1968."

"Who the heck was Peter Halat?" Sue wondered. "And what does he have to do with lost money?"

Ellen took her pendulum from her purse. "Why don't we try to ask the spirits here to help us?"

Before her friends could respond, a car appeared on the path and headed toward them, its headlights shining directly on them.

Ellen tucked her pendulum back into her purse, aware that not everyone appreciated the summoning of spirits.

"Maybe we should come back another time," Tanya said.

"The cemetery's closing!" an old man shouted from his car window as he passed.

Ellen and her friends giggled.

Sue arched a brow. "He sure was friendly."

"That was your nice southern hospitality right there," Ellen added with a wink.

CHAPTER SEVEN

The Third Floor

Once they were upstairs in their summer rental, Ellen fed Mo, changed into her pajamas, and met her friends on the balcony for margaritas. Although it was hot, there was a strong breeze that made the night air more palatable this evening. As she ate her warmed-up burger from the Hard Rock Café on the patio table with her friends, Ellen squinted at the lighthouse, wondering if she would see the shadow woman whom she believed to be Angelique Fayard.

"At least I broke even today," Tanya remarked after a while.

"You're still down five hundred from yesterday," Sue reminded her.

"You don't have to tell me, Sue. I'm aware."

"I don't know what you're worried about," Ellen said. "It's not like you're having trouble making ends meet. The gold money and the oil money have been good to us."

"Money isn't everything," Sue began, "but it sure helps keep you in touch with your kids."

Tanya chuckled and shook her head.

"Ain't that the truth," Ellen agreed with a laugh. "Lane's already hitting me up for a fancy-shmancy breast pump for Maya. It's over five hundred dollars. Can you believe that? We didn't have anything like that when we had our babies. Do mothers really need them, do you think?"

Sue shrugged. "I don't know, but I wouldn't mind having a fancy-shmancy breast pump—not one that pumps stuff out but pumps stuff *up*, if you know what I mean." Sue lifted her large breasts so that they stood straight out from her chest.

Tanya threw her head back and guffawed.

Ellen nearly choked on her frozen margarita.

After a beat, Ellen asked, "What if Isabel wasn't talking about hitting the jackpot on the slots?"

Tanya raised her brows. "Oh, you think it's the ghost's lost money?"

Ellen shrugged. "I don't know. Maybe. I Googled Peter Halat, and although I can't find anything on Senior, it seems that his son was once the mayor of Biloxi and was involved in a scandal back in the eighties and nineties."

Sue picked up her phone from the table. "I've tried Googling 'Biloxi lost money' and 'Biloxi legends,' but so far, all I get is the Hotel Legends, which, by the way, is also on Beach Boulevard."

"That reminds me," Tanya began, "after we check out the Beauvoir tomorrow, I want to go see the White House Hotel on the way back. It's just west of the Old Biloxi Cemetery. It's one of the few buildings on the coast to have survived Hurricane Katrina, and it's been around since the 1800s."

"I wonder if Angelique showed us Senior's grave to tell us something about his son," Ellen pondered as she took another sip of her margarita.

"Don't forget to take in the view, you guys," Tanya chastised as she waved a hand in front of her. A half-moon and sparkling stars shimmered on the sea tonight. "The whole point in coming on this trip was to get away and relax."

Ellen pointed a finger at Tanya. "You forget how good I am at multitasking."

"Yeah," Sue agreed. "Ellen can sneeze and pee at the same time."

Ellen shook her head and was trying to think of a clever comeback when she was startled by another thud overhead.

"Not again!" Tanya groaned.

"I can't believe Brenda still hasn't called you back," Sue said. "If you're going to have renters, you need to be available."

"Or, if you can't," Ellen began, "hire a management firm."

"Exactly," Sue agreed.

"Should we call 9-1-1?" Tanya wondered.

"It won't do any good if we can't get ahold of Brenda," Sue pointed out.

"Unless the officers hear the noise, too," Ellen argued.

Another thud came—louder than the last.

"That's it." Sue jumped from the patio chair and went straight for her purse. Pulling out her gun, she asked, "Who's coming with me?"

"For heaven's sake," Tanya said. "Enough with the gun already."

"One of these days you're going to thank me, Tanya."

Ellen and Mo followed her friends inside. "I'm pretty sure that day has come and gone. We're grateful, Sue, but sometimes you look a bit trigger happy. You can't blame us for preaching caution." Ellen closed the balcony doors behind them.

"Have your phone ready to call the police, just in case," Sue warned as she charged through the door to the stairwell. Tanya followed, hanging back a few feet.

Ellen stood on the landing between the second and third floors, not knowing what to do.

When Sue knocked on the upstairs door, which was directly over the door to their second-floor unit, something pounded back in reply, shaking the door in its frame.

Ellen screamed. It sounded like the others did too, but Ellen, who was frozen there on the landing, her eyes wide, her heart pounding, wasn't sure.

"What the heck?" Sue muttered.

"I'm calling 9-1-1," Tanya said loud enough for an intruder to hear.

"You better get out of there, if you know what's good for you," Sue warned as she took several steps back. "I have a gun, and I'm not afraid to use it."

"If only the door wasn't locked," Ellen groaned.

Sue quietly crept up and tried the knob. As the knob turned and the door opened inward, Sue gave them a look of astonishment, mouthing, "Oh, my gawd!" as she raced down the stairs toward Ellen.

"What on earth?" Ellen headed down the stairs, too, followed by her friends, but then, barking ferociously, Moseby ran past her up the stairs and entered the third floor.

"Moseby! Get back here!" Ellen cried.

She rushed up the steps after her dog, her heart pounding a million beats per minute. As soon as she entered the room, she was accosted by cobwebs. Thick dust encroached on her lungs. She nearly tripped on a loose floorboard as she made her way toward the sound of Mo barking. It was obvious no one had been up there in quite some time. Why had Brenda lied to them?

"Moseby?" Ellen called as she glanced around the dark and dingy parlor, illuminated by nothing more than the moonlight washing in from the front floor-to-ceiling windows. Mo's bark had become a low growl, but he was nowhere in sight.

Using the light from her phone, she made her way past a fireplace with a cracked and rotting wood façade. The drywall above it and on the walls and ceiling peeled back in places, exposing shiplap. Some of the wooden floorboards beneath her were loose, and an old wooden dining table lay on its side, the chairs only a heap of rubble in the middle of the room. "Moseby? Where are you. boy?"

He had stopped growling.

"Ellen?" Sue called from the door. "Oh, my gawd. This place is a disaster."

"You're telling me. Do you see Moseby?"

"No. Which way did he go?"

A door to the right of Ellen creaked as it slowly swung open, revealing a bathroom. It had an old-fashioned claw tub at the far end, peeling paint on a beadboard ceiling, and gray, speckled linoleum floors.

"Moseby?" she called as she entered the room, feeling as though a negative force was luring her in.

The bath was attached to a bedroom, where she saw a curtain move. She inched her way inside and pulled the curtain up, but Mo was nowhere to be seen. The old iron bedframe behind her, holding a bare mattress, creaked. Wondering if he was hiding beneath the bed, Ellen crouched down on her hands and knees.

"Moseby?"

She was afraid to look, terrified of what might be lurking underneath, but, worried about her dog, she forced her head down to the dusty, old floor. Relief swept through her when there was no monster to be found, but her relief was short-lived when the closet door, on the other side of the bed from her, creaked as it slowly swung open.

"Mo?"

Ellen climbed to her feet, walked around the bed, and looked inside the closet. There was nothing in there but a big cardboard box about three feet tall and wide. Before turning away to continue her search for Mo, she thought she saw the box move.

She froze in place and held her breath, waiting to see if it would move again. When it didn't, she continued through the room into a dark hallway.

"Ellen?" Sue called from the front parlor—the first room Ellen had entered on the third floor. "Where are you?"

"I'm over here, in the hall. Do you see Mo?"

"Not yet. He's not in the dumbwaiter, thank goodness."

"Where's Tanya?"

"She's waiting for the police downstairs."

Sue poked her head through a door at the end of the hallway.

"There you are," Ellen said. "You check that room, and I'll check this one."

Ellen entered another bedroom. This one also had an iron bedframe, but the mattress was gone. There weren't any curtains either, but there was a closet, and the door was ajar.

"Moseby?"

She heard him whimpering.

"There you are!" She opened the door and found him in the furthest back corner. "It's okay, boy." She scooped him up and cried, "Found him!"

As she followed Sue down the hall to the front room, she heard a scratching sound behind her. Mo heard it, too, and growled.

"What was that?" Sue asked.

To Ellen, it sounded like the cardboard box scraping along the wooden floor.

"Let's get out of here," she said. "The police can take it from here."

As they rushed to leave, they were shocked when the door, which Sue had left ajar, slammed shut.

"Tanya?" Sue raced to the door and attempted to open it. Looking at Ellen, she cried, "It won't open."

"What? It's got to." Ellen rushed beside her friend and twisted the knob, but it wouldn't move.

"Is there a key?" Sue searched the floor. "Maybe there's a key."

A pounding on the door from the other side made both friends jump back. Moseby continued to growl in Ellen's arms. There seemed to be something in the bathroom that was bothering him—or maybe it was the cardboard box in the adjacent room.

"Open up. It's the police."

"We're trying!" Sue cried. "The door won't open!"

Ellen heard another scratching sound. Was that box moving?

"Help!" she cried to the police—her throat suddenly dry and as scratchy as sandpaper. "Break it down and get us out of here!"

"Stand back, away from the door," one of the officers instructed.

Ellen watched as the door shook with three strikes or kicks from the officer behind it before it finally yielded and swung open.

"Go downstairs and lock yourselves in your unit," he instructed them.

With Mo still growling in her arms, Ellen hastened after Sue down the steps, where Tanya was waiting for them.

"We're to wait inside," Sue told Tanya.

Once they were safe in their own unit, Ellen hugged her dog close as tears welled in her eyes. "Don't do that to me again, Moseby-Mo. You scared the living daylights out of me!"

From the open door of her bedroom, Ellen could hear the German shepherd barking. She went to her bedroom window and looked down at him. His face was turned up to the third floor, and he was barking nonstop.

Did he and Moseby sense something evil on the third floor?

CHAPTER EIGHT

The Box

Friday night, after the police had found nothing on the third floor—no sign of a varmint, a vagrant, or an intruder of any kind—Ellen and her friends tried once again to reach the homeowners and still had no luck. This time, however, Tanya left a long message about what had happened—about the door opening, about Moseby running inside with Ellen and Sue following, about the police being called, and about how obvious it had been that no one—not even the homeowners themselves—had been up there in quite some time. Tanya demanded an explanation and the courtesy of a return call, threatening to leave a bad review on Trip Advisor and to report the experience to the Better Business Bureau.

The three friends were once again in the main living area, trying to recover from what had happened as Tanya finished her call.

Once she'd hung up, she said, "Hopefully that gets an answer out of them."

"I would hope so," Ellen agreed. "I have a feeling they know more than they're letting on."

"It's got to be something paranormal," Sue remarked. "Good job, Tanya. I didn't know you had it in you."

"Oh, stop," Tanya said.

"There was a box in one of the bedroom closets," Ellen mentioned. "I thought it moved."

"Why didn't you tell the police?" Tanya demanded.

"I thought I had imagined it. And I very well may have. Besides, I was too flummoxed to tell them. Everything was happening so fast."

"Don't blame Ellen, Tanya. You wouldn't even go up there."

"Someone had to wait for the police," Tanya insisted.

"I bet they would have found their way up there without your help," Sue remarked.

"It doesn't matter," Ellen said, trying to stop the conflict from escalating. She didn't want her friends to say anything they would later regret. "We're all okay, and that's what's important."

"But are we okay?" Tanya asked. "Are we really? What if there's something evil in that box?"

"Priestess Isabel said we'd be okay as long as we didn't cross the boundary," Sue reminded them. "If we stay down here, we should be fine."

"You laughed at the idea of it being the third floor when Ellen mentioned it," Tanya pointed out. "Besides, you *did* cross it, and now we're screwed."

Sue narrowed her eyes. "Should we have left Moseby up there alone?"

Ellen sighed. "Come on, let's not argue. We've got our *gris gris* and our tourmaline rings. I'll spritz the rooms with holy water and pour salt on the threshold. That should protect us for the night."

"It's freezing in here." Tanya got up and grabbed her sweater from one of the dining chairs and put it on. "Aren't you guys cold?"

"I have hot flashes too often to ever get cold," Ellen said.

Sue wiped a bead of sweat from her brow. "Same. You'd think I'd lose weight with how much I sweat."

"And as hot as I get, that heat should burn some of this fat, shouldn't it?" Ellen pinched the spare tire around her waist.

"It should be good for *something*," Sue agreed.

A loud thud on the floor overhead made all three ladies jump. Mo looked at Ellen and whined.

Ellen jumped to her feet and pointed to the ceiling. "It's coming from the place where I saw the box. There must be something in it."

"Like an animal?" Tanya asked hopefully.

Ellen shook her head. "It was sealed with packing tape."

"How closely did you look at it?" Sue wondered. "Could an animal have chewed through the back or bottom of it?"

Ellen tilted her head. "Wouldn't the police have noticed?"

"Not necessarily." Tanya crossed her arms. "Oh, gosh. I'm really hoping for a rat right now."

The thud came again.

"I'm not going to be able to get a lick of sleep," Sue complained. "I say we go up there and investigate. We've already crossed the boundary anyway."

"I guess if it *is* a rat or a raccoon, we could shoo it away," Tanya conceded.

"Or shoot it," Sue put in.

"And if it's a haunted object?" Ellen wondered aloud. "Do we throw it in the ocean?"

"I like that idea," Tanya said. "Except that Priestess—"

Sue stood up and crossed the room for her purse. "We know what she said, Tanya. You don't have to remind us."

Tanya stood up, too, as Sue took out her gun. "So, you're just going to ignore her warning?"

"Not ignore. Take it under advisement. I'll be careful. Besides, like I said, we've already crossed it once. Are you coming, Ellen?"

"Let me put Mo in my bedroom."

Ellen put Moseby on the queen bed and stroked his fur. "You stay here and be a good boy." She took the bottle of holy water from her bag on the dresser and sprayed a few squirts in the room. "You'll be safe in here." Then, taking the bottle with her, she closed the bedroom door and followed Sue to the stairs.

"I hope you two know what you're doing."

"Keep an eye out for Mo, will you, Tanya?" Ellen asked. "And be ready to call the police if we don't come back in ten minutes."

Tanya shook her head and sucked in her lips. "Okay. If you say so. Gosh, I wish you weren't going up there."

"I want to enjoy myself while we're here," Sue insisted, "not cower in fear the whole time. Plus, I need my beauty sleep. All this—" she waved a hand over her body, "doesn't happen unless I get at least eight hours of good shut eye."

Without another word, Sue opened the door to the stairwell and led the way to the third floor. Ellen followed with her holy water, silently saying a prayer.

As they reached the door to the third floor, Ellen heard someone or something on the stairs behind her. The hair on the back of her neck stood on end.

"Oh, God," she whispered.

Sue glanced back at her, her eyes falling on something or someone behind Ellen. "Tanya? I thought you weren't coming."

Ellen sighed with relief. "You scared the holy crap out of me."

"Sorry. I couldn't let you two go alone."

Sue laughed.

Defensive, Tanya asked, "What's so funny?"

"Ellen. She thinks her crap is holy."

The three friends giggled as they approached the door. Sue turned the knob. As it had before, the door opened inward. The three friends exchanged looks of surprise and dread.

"It's like something wants us to go in there," Ellen whispered.

With her gun out in front of her, Sue stepped inside and looked around the room as Ellen and Tanya stood behind her.

"Where did you say that box was?" Sue asked.

"That way." Ellen pointed to the bathroom. "Through that bath to the bedroom. It's in the closet."

Sue kept the gun out, as she led the way. Ellen supposed it gave them all a sense of security, even though it really wasn't useful.

If they found a varmint, Ellen and Tanya would not let Sue shoot it. And if they found something paranormal—well, you couldn't shoot a ghost with a gun. Holy water, on the other hand, was a different matter, and Ellen was ready.

Ellen tried switching on the bathroom light and was surprised when it came on. So, there was electricity. There just weren't any lightbulbs but this one.

When they reached the bedroom, the box was no longer inside the closet but out a few feet beside the bed.

"I wonder if the cops moved it," Ellen said. "It *was* in the closet."

"Open it while I point the gun at it," Sue ordered.

"I think I need scissors or a knife," Ellen said.

"Will this work?' Tanya pulled a nail file from her blue jean pocket. "I was filing my nails earlier."

"Take this spritzer and be ready to spray," Ellen instructed Tanya of the holy water.

Ellen took the file and cut the tape on the sides and down the middle before slowly lifting open the flaps of the box.

"What do you see?" Tanya wanted to know.

"Another box," Ellen said as she cautiously lifted it out and put it on the bed.

It, too, was sealed with packing tape, so she performed the same procedure on it as she had on the first.

"Another box," Ellen said. "This feels like a Chinese puzzle."

This time, however, as Ellen touched the third box, she felt a jolt of electricity pulse through her fingers. She flinched and jumped back, startled.

"What happened?" Sue asked.

Tanya put a hand on Ellen's shoulder. "Are you okay?"

"It shocked me." She grabbed the holy water from Tanya and sprayed the box with it, but nothing happened.

Tanya removed her sweater and used it like oven mitts to lift the box out of the second box and lay it on the bed.

Ellen was impressed. She took a deep breath. "Here goes nothing." Then using the file, she opened the box.

Inside was a book—a black, leather planner with the year 1987 embossed in gold on the bottom corner of the front cover.

Ellen took Tanya's sweater and used it to lift the planner from the box. It shook violently in her hands and dropped to the floor, its pages flapping like an injured bird attempting to fly.

"Ahhh!' Tanya cried.

"Oh, my gawd!" Sue was pointing her gun at it.

"Don't shoot it!" Ellen warned. "Put your gun away . . . please, Sue."

Sue returned it to her purse, which was strapped over her shoulder. "Now what?"

Ellen leaned over the flapping book and, using Tanya's sweater, picked it up by the leather cover and laid it on the bed, holding it open with both hands. There was an inscription on the inside cover: *To the Honorable Judge Vincent Sherry. Your Friend, Pete Halat.*

"Don't touch that!" a woman's voice carried into the room.

The three friends flinched and turned, finding a couple in their early sixties standing in the doorway.

"Brenda?" Tanya asked.

"That thing is dangerous," Brenda's husband warned. "Put it back in the box."

Believing the planner might shed some light on the mysterious force possessing it, Ellen quickly combed through its pages despite the book's strange movements. "What do you mean by dangerous?"

"It's possessed," Brenda claimed. "You wouldn't believe what we've been through with that thing."

Not seeing anything but meeting dates and times, Ellen closed the book as it wriggled and flapped in her hands and, with Tanya's help, returned it to the smallest box. Together, they put the small box into the medium one, and the medium one into the large one, just as they'd found it, minus the tape. As soon as Ellen set the box in the closet, it trembled violently.

Sue slammed the closet door shut. "Let's get the heck out of here."

All five of them rushed from the third floor to the second-floor unit.

As Ellen went to get Mo from her room, she heard Tanya say, "I think you owe us an explanation."

"We better sit down." Brenda took one of the dining chairs at the wooden table with her husband. "This is John, by the way."

With Mo in her arms, Ellen took a wingback chair beside Sue. "Nice to meet you."

Tanya curled up on the chaise lounge. "Nice to meet you, but we're so confused. What's going on?"

Brenda cleared her throat. "We bought this property in 2006—nearly a year after Hurricane Katrina."

"It was a mess," John explained. "The roof was gone, most of the windows needed replacing, and all the dry wall on this floor was either rotten or missing. But the frame had held up, so that's why we bought it."

"It took us a year just to clear all the rubble off the property," Brenda said. "It took another year for us to reframe parts of the structure, have a new roof put on, and add the electrical and new plumbing and drywall on the lower unit. We couldn't afford to do it all at once, so we started with the second floor, renting it out in 2010, so that we could earn revenue on it our while we worked on the top floor."

"We didn't discover the planner until sometime in 2012," John said. "We had lost our renter, and I had just begun work on the attic when it fell from a rafter and hit me on the head."

Brenda flapped a hand through the air. "We recognized the name, and being from Biloxi, we knew about the murders. We immediately mailed the planner to the police."

Ellen straightened her back. "What murders?"

John seemed surprised that they hadn't heard about them. "Back in 1987, a judge and his wife by the name of Vincent and Margaret Sherry were killed. It looked like a professional hit. It took over a decade to piece together a case, but no one knows what really happened, and no one was ever found guilty of their murders."

"The planner was the only thing missing from the crime scene," Brenda added. "When we found it, we knew it was important evidence."

John folded his arms across his chest. "We mailed it anonymously because we didn't want to get involved."

"But a week later, when we went upstairs to clear out the rubble, there it was, still in the envelope," Brenda said. "I mailed it again, and it came right back."

"That's when we knew we weren't dealing with anything natural," John stated. "So, more out of fear really, I threw the book as far as I could into the gulf."

"But it came back," Brenda said. "And it wasn't even wet. It looked exactly as it had when we'd first discovered it."

Ellen glanced at her friends. "That's incredible."

"Next, I ripped it to shreds," John explained. "I burnt part of it and threw away other pieces of it in different trash bins all over town."

"But it came back," Sue said.

"Yep," Brenda confirmed. "Only now it seemed angry."

"I boxed it up as best as I could and left it in the room where it had always returned," John said.

"Later, when we returned to the third floor, we couldn't open the door," Brenda said. "It was as if the book had locked us out. After hiring a locksmith to open it for us, we got the help of a priest, a team of paranormal investigators, and a medium, and no one could help us."

"As long as we stayed away from the third floor, everything seemed fine," John added. "Renting out this unit was helping us to finally recoup some of our investment. We've put off finishing the third floor indefinitely."

"This is the first incident we've had in almost ten years," Brenda stated. "But we've completely avoided the top floor."

"Why did you lie to us about checking things out the other day?" Tanya wanted to know.

"We tried to go up there, but we couldn't unlock the door," John explained. "I was afraid that if I broke it open, the book would cause more problems for you—for all of us—so I left it alone, hoping the sudden movement had been a fluke, and the book would settle down."

"You should have been honest with us," Tanya insisted.

Brenda laughed nervously. "How do you tell such a story to renters? I'm surprised you've let us get this far without calling the cops on us and trying to have us admitted into a psychiatric facility."

"We're paranormal investigators," Ellen explained.

"We have the gift," Sue added, "which is probably why that book reached out to us."

Brenda and her husband raised their brows as hopeful expressions crossed their faces.

"Can you help us?" Brenda asked.

"We'll refund your money and have you here indefinitely if you can," John added.

"We should get the refund regardless," Tanya pointed out.

"Of course," Brenda said as her face turned red.

Ellen could tell it would be a financial hit to the couple to lose the rent money. The house hadn't come cheaply. "Do you know who owned this house at the time of the murders?"

"We bought it from a man called Brashear," Brenda said, "but he lived in Florida and had been renting the house for at least ten years. I don't know if he ever lived here or who owned it before him."

Sue lifted her chin and narrowed her eyes. "Didn't you ask him about the book?"

"No," John said sternly. "We didn't want anyone to know we had it."

"You think whoever killed the Sherrys is still a threat?" Ellen asked.

"Yes, I do." John tapped his fist on the dining table. "In fact, I wouldn't go looking for answers about how the book ended up where it did, if I were you. I'd just find a way to banish whatever demon is possessing it."

"We'll do what we can while we're here," Sue said. "But we *will* need more information if we're to figure out who or what is haunting the planner."

"There's an excellent book about the murders called *Mississippi Mud*," Brenda said. "And any internet search should bring up good results."

Ellen stood up with Mo in her arms and stifled a yawn. "We'll get to work and keep you posted."

"Oh, it's late, hun, we should go," Brenda said. "Are you sure you're okay staying here?"

"We'll manage," Sue promised, "now that we have a better idea of what we're up against."

"Thank you for your willingness to help," John said as he followed his wife to the door. "We'll be better about making ourselves available if you need to reach us."

The couple left, and the three friends collapsed in their chairs.

"What a night," Tanya complained. "I'm wiped."

Although Ellen was exhausted, the wheels in her head were spinning. "We need to find out everything we can about those murders. Would y'all mind skipping the sight-seeing tomorrow to read instead?"

"What if we read on the beach?" Tanya suggested.

Ellen and Sue glanced at each other and nodded.

"Sounds like a good compromise," Sue said. "But before we go to bed, I'm putting salt on the threshold. Ellen, you spray the rooms. Whatever is possessing that book has got to be powerful to have found its way back after so many efforts at getting rid of it."

"Better make circles of protection around our beds, too," Tanya advised. "The last thing we need is another possession."

CHAPTER NINE

The Sherry Murders

Saturday morning, after buying a few snacks and margarita supplies at a nearby grocery store, Ellen and her friends used the dumbwaiter from the breezeway to send their groceries to the second floor.

"It works!" Tanya cried as Ellen and Sue followed her into the kitchen.

"Everything make it up okay?" Sue asked.

Tanya had already started moving the grocery bags from the dumbwaiter to the kitchen counter. "They're all here."

Another loud thud sounded overhead, just above the dumbwaiter.

"Hells bells," Sue said. "Let's hurry and get to the beach."

Ellen and her friends rented wooden loungers again on Biloxi Beach and used their phones to scour the internet for information about the murders of Vincent and Margaret Sherry. The sun was bright in a cloudless sky, and a pleasant breeze kept the air from stifling them. The gulf, as a result, appeared as restless as they were as they sipped cold mimosas with their heads down.

Moseby was kept busy on the lounger beside Ellen with a chicken-flavored treat that would require at least one full day of licking and chewing before he would finish it off.

"Listen to this," Tanya said suddenly. "Margaret Sherry had recently given up her seat on the city council to run on the Republican ticket for mayor against the incumbent Democrat, Gerald Blessey, and lost. This article says they hated one another. She accused him of being complicit with the criminal underworld, and he accused her of being a racist and a bigot, arguing that her criminal-defense-attorney husband profited more from crime than he did."

"Wow," Ellen remarked. "Was Blessey a suspect?"

Tanya shrugged. "It seems the police thought Vincent was the target and not Margaret."

"That's what I'm reading," Sue chimed in. "This article talks about a scheme run by an inmate by the name of Kirksey Nix targeting gay men with fake personal ads. The ads described handsome, lonely, gay inmates looking for a stable partner for their upcoming release from prison. Once a man was on the hook, he was preyed upon with requests for money to help with fines, moving expenses, health costs, and other bogus financial emergencies, which the smitten victims were only too glad to pay, believing they were helping someone they had come to love."

Ellen snapped her fingers. "I remember that. The Lonely Hearts Scam. I heard about it back when I was in college. They stole hundreds of thousands of dollars from their victims, didn't they?"

"Yes, maybe as much as five million. And Pete Halat was Nix's attorney," Sue said. "He oversaw Nix's finances, so when the scam money turned up missing, Nix questioned Halat. Halat pointed a finger at his partner, Vincent Sherry, and that's why the mafia murdered him."

"The mafia?" Ellen repeated.

"The Dixie Mafia," Sue clarified. "This article says that they aren't connected by family like the Italian mafia but are composed mainly of white Southerners based in Biloxi, operating throughout the Southern United States since at least the late 1960s. They move stolen merchandise, illegal alcohol, and illegal drugs and were historically involved in strip clubs, prostitution rings, and gambling dens before gambling was legalized in Biloxi."

"So, the mafia went after Vincent because his partner Pete accused him of stealing their money?" Ellen asked.

Sue nodded. "That's what this article suggests. It says that a private detective hired by the Sherrys' children spoke with a member of the Dixie Mafia who was imprisoned for life. Inmate Bobby Joe Fabian revealed to Detective Armistead that Kirksey Nix planted his girlfriend, Sheri LaRa Sharpe, at the Halat and Sherry law firm to run his Lonely Hearts Scam. When Nix discovered that the money from his scam was missing, he demanded a meeting with Halat, who blamed it on Vincent. Mike Gillich, Jr., an associate of Kirskey Nix and the godfather of Biloxi who ran the Golden Nugget Casino and various strip clubs and gambling dens, also met with Halat and was told the same thing: Vincent must have taken the money. Bobby Joe Fabian named John Ransom as the hitman hired by Nix to kill Vincent."

"Was any of that proven?" Tanya asked. "Because this article highlights Margaret Sherry's commitment to cleaning up crime in Biloxi. She was set on exposing the corruption. It seems to me that the mafia might have wanted to silence her."

"Maybe it was a twofer," Sue suggested. "They were both targets."

Ellen lifted her finger. "I found something. This article says what played out in the courts: 'The trial began on Sept. 30, 1991, four years after the Sherry murders and just before the statute of limitations would have run out.' The article goes on to say that Nix was sentenced to fifteen years in prison, added to the life sentence he was already serving. Gillich also got fifteen years. Ransom swore he hadn't killed Vincent or Margaret but had knowledge of the murders and would cooperate for a deal. He told investigators that he had refused to kill a woman, so he passed it off to another hitman. He was sentenced to ten years. And Sharpe was sentenced to one year and one week in prison for her part in the lonely-hearts scam and wire fraud." Ellen looked up. "But no one was found guilty of murder."

"Wait," Sue said, waving her hand excitedly. "This article on WLOX dot com reports that in 1994, Gillich cooperated with the FBI for a shorter sentence. He said Halat told Nix that Vincent Sherry stole the money to save his own life. Nix and Gillich ordered a hit on Vincent. Nix and Gillich said they would split the cost of the hitman. They were going to hire Ransom but decided on a man named Thomas Holcomb. Later, they said Halat did offer to help pay, but Gillich supposedly told him it was taken care of. Margaret Sherry's murder was just a bonus and a precaution. It says that 'in 1996, the government indicted Nix, Sharpe, Hallat, and Holcomb on dozens of charges, including racketeering, fraud, conspiracy to commit wire fraud, money laundering, and conspiracy to obstruct justice.' Further down, it says that 'the Sherry murders are technically still open cases as no one was ever charged with their murders, and no one knows what really happened to the money.'"

Ellen's eyes widened as she sat up in her chair. "The lost money!"

"The lost money!" Tanya echoed.

Invigorated by the prospect of solving a decades-old mystery involving hundreds of thousands of lost dollars and an open homicide case, the three friends spent the morning on the beach reading everything they could find on the Sherry murders before taking a break at one o'clock to lunch at the Palace Casino buffet. Over freshly-boiled and fried shrimp, grilled fish, fried okra, creamy mashed potatoes, and crisp salad greens, they put together a timeline of important events.

Tanya took a sip of her water. "Vincent and Margaret were found dead in their home on Wednesday, September 16, 1987. Vincent was found in the den and Margaret upstairs in her bedroom. Both appeared to have been shot point blank multiple times."

Ellen shuddered. "How awful."

"They were found by Pete Halat," Sue added. "This was Vincent's partner. He later became the mayor. Vincent, being a judge, didn't show up to court on Wednesday morning. Vincent's court clerk called Pete, wondering where Vincent was. When Pete couldn't get

Vincent on the phone, he asked his wife to drive over and knock on the door. The wife said no one answered but both cars were there, so Pete took his colleague Charles Leger to the house, discovered Vincent, and called the cops, who later found Margaret."

"But what led up to the day they were killed?" Ellen wondered. "I think I read that the Sherrys were planning to visit their younger daughter at her college on the Tuesday before they were found."

"I read that, too," Sue said. "They were going to Baton Rouge to see her and to have cataracts removed from one of their dogs."

"But they never made it out of town," Ellen said as she offered Moseby a bite of fish.

Tanya lifted a finger. "It says here that 'on the Monday before they were found, Vincent went jogging, got his hair cut at Keesler Air Force base, and gassed up his old station wagon. Margaret went shopping and planned a United Daughters of the Confederacy convention, which she would be chairing the following month.'" Tanya took another sip of her water. "The Daughters of the Confederacy? Isn't that a white supremacist group?"

"I'm not sure," Ellen admitted.

"I think they devote themselves to maintaining the memory of their Confederate husbands and sons with cemetery and memorial upkeep," Sue said. "I don't think they're white supremacists."

"I don't know about that," Tanya said dubiously. "I remember reading that they are as devoted to the old values of the confederacy as they are the memorials." She quickly added, "Oh, listen to this: 'Margaret Sherry told three different friends in telephone conversations that she had been working with the FBI to expose a crime ring in Biloxi and that she would be putting Gerald Blessey—the mayor at that time—behind bars.'"

"Wow," Sue said. "Maybe you're right and whoever killed them was after Margaret. Maybe the courts got it wrong."

"It sure sounds that way," Ellen agreed.

Sue put her fork down and leaned over her phone. "This article supports that theory. It says that days after the bodies were found, Lynn, the Sherrys' older daughter, said that her mother had claimed that she was going to blow the lid off crime in Biloxi—that she had something big. Lynn reported that her mother had said that she just hoped they wouldn't come after her children."

"I don't understand why the police didn't work the case from that angle," Ellen said before taking another bite of creamy mashed potatoes. "It sounds like their whole case hinged on what members of the Dixie Mafia claimed. What if they were lying? And what if Blessey was, as Margaret claimed, associated with them?"

"It seems the police couldn't find anything on Blessey," Sue reported.

"I just found an article about him." Ellen scrolled through her phone and read, "'Blessey was considered the most liberal elected official in Mississippi, pursuing progressive reforms and government activism that would create opportunity and safety nets for the poor, which heavily skewed black. Blessey was a champion for civil rights and was beloved by the black community, unlike Margaret Sherry, who opposed a city holiday honoring the birth of Martin Luther King, Jr.'"

"So, she *was* racist," Tanya accused.

Sue put a hand on her waist. "Just because she didn't support Martin Luther King Day, that doesn't mean she was racist."

"I guess you're right," Tanya admitted.

"I know I am. And if I had a dime for every time someone said that to me, I'd be a rich woman."

Ellen guffawed. "Sue, you *are* a rich woman."

"I know," Sue said with a giggle.

The three friends returned to reading on their phones.

"I'm skimming an interview with the older daughter, Lynn," Sue said before popping a piece of fried okra into her mouth. "She claimed that when she asked Pete who he thought the killer was, he advised her and her siblings to 'drop it,' because nothing could bring their parents back."

"Why would he say that unless he was guilty or knew something?" Ellen wondered.

"Maybe he suspected that his client Kirksey Nix ordered the hit," Tanya pointed out. "Maybe he was just worried for the kids."

Ellen could see that. "Okay, good point. So, you're saying Gillich could have lied about Halat's involvement, maybe to make his information seem more valuable to the police as he was seeking a shorter sentence." Then she added, "Oh, listen to this. It's a list of initial suspects . . . a few of Vincent's clients—including a cocaine-smuggling preacher, a Chicago mobster, a cocaine smuggler called Diamond Betsy, and the king of Biloxi's strip, Mike Gillich. They even investigated the older son, Eric, for a while, because people didn't think his grief was sincere and someone claimed to have seen him in town on the evening of the day the bodies were found when he should have been in Florida. The article says that while the police were investigating Vincent's old clients and one of his sons, the citizens of Biloxi turned suspicious eyes to their mayor, but the police quickly dismissed him as a suspect when the FBI denied that they'd been working with Margaret to convict him. Pete Halat was briefly questioned, but there was no motive. He was their best friend and stood to lose money with his law partner deceased."

"Except that, two years later, he became the mayor of Biloxi," Sue pointed out. "That could have been his motive right there. And what if he was the one who stole the lost money? Making Vincent the scapegoat could have been his motive."

"Good points, Sue, but the police never found evidence that Pete had the money, and listen to this," Ellen continued. "'When the younger daughter, Leslie, went looking for her father's appointment book and discovered it missing, the investigators had their first lead: the murderer must have known his victims, for why else would he steal the book? The book undoubtedly named the last person to see the Sherrys alive, and that person was their murderer.'"

Ellen looked up at her friends. "You know what this means, don't you?"

As if he knew, too, Moseby whined.

"Yep," Sue said.

Tanya groaned. "We have to go back up to the third floor and get that damn book."

After lunch, they returned to their summer house and geared themselves up to face whatever was haunting the third floor. Wearing their *gris gris* bags and tourmaline rings, they also carried salt and holy water and, despite objections from Ellen and Tanya, Sue carried her gun.

Mo had been left on Ellen's bed with the door closed and a line of salt poured on the threshold. He seemed happy to go back to licking and chewing his chicken-flavored treat.

When they reached the top of the stairs, the third-floor door slowly swung open. Ellen at first thought the homeowners were there.

"Brenda?" she called, as she followed Sue inside with Tanya on her heels. "John?"

"It doesn't look like anyone's here," Sue remarked.

"Do you think the book wants us to come in?" Tanya asked.

"It sure looks like it." Ellen led the way through the bath to the adjacent bedroom, where the boxes lay on the floor and the planner lay open on the bed.

Cautiously, Ellen leaned over the book and found it to be open to the month of September, when the murders had occurred.

Sue gasped with astonishment. "It was waiting for us. It wants us to know."

Squinting, Ellen read what had been written in for the Monday evening before the bodies were found. "Take-out dinner with Sister Anna Celeste at Sisters of Mercy?"

Tanya wrinkled her nose. "Does this mean they were murdered by a nun?"

Without touching the book, Ellen glanced at the other appointments that month. The planner confirmed Vincent's plans to have his hair cut on Monday morning and to visit the vet and his daughter on Tuesday. There was nothing written in for Saturday and Sunday. On Friday, he'd had lunch with Pete, but that seemed to be a common occurrence on Fridays, so why would that information be worthy of stealing the appointment book?

Sue tapped a finger to her chin. "I wonder if Sister Anna Celeste is still alive."

As if it was pleased by this statement, the book jiggled on the bed.

The three friends gawked.

While Sue searched for information about the nun on her phone, Ellen sprayed the room with holy water. "Tanya, why don't you pour a circle of salt around the book, just to be safe?"

When Tanya neared the bed, the planner leapt up and slapped the shaker from Tanya's hand. Tanya screamed and flailed her arms and ran from the room.

Sue and Ellen quickly followed, Ellen's heart about to explode in her chest.

Safely in their own unit, Ellen tried to catch her breath. "What the heck just happened?"

CHAPTER TEN

Sisters of Mercy

Once they'd recovered from their encounter with the haunted book, Ellen and her friends took Mo east on Beach Boulevard past the Beau Rivage, turning just before Mary Mahoney's Old French House to, of all streets, Fayard Street, in search of the Sisters of Mercy Convent. They were surprised to find a plain-looking, red brick, ranch-style house rather than an institutional-looking building. As there was no signage, only the crucifix on the front door, painted green, gave any indication that this might be the right place. The green door had two large windows on either side of it, each trimmed with white shutters. That was the extent of the building's décor. There was no landscaping except for a lawn of struggling grass. There was a car parked in the driveaway on the right side of the house in front of a white garage door. Across the street from the house was a parking lot, and just past it was a seafood market.

"Is this it?" Tanya asked doubtfully.

"It's the right address," Sue confirmed as she pulled up to the curb. "And it looks like someone might be home."

The homes on the street were separated by chain-link fences. While most of these were limited to the back yards, a few of them had fencing in the front, too. The house to the left was one of them. To the right was an empty lot. Ellen wondered if there had once been a house there that had become another casualty of Hurricane Katrina.

Ellen climbed from the back seat of the Pilot with Moseby in his cloth pooch carrier. "Let's check it out."

As they walked up the driveaway and onto the sidewalk, Sue muttered, "The sisters certainly don't waste money on beautification, do they?"

"I'm sure they have more important things to worry about," Tanya chastised. "Like caring for the sick and the poor."

"I'm sure," Sue said just before she rapped on the front door.

While they waited, Tanya whispered, "Do we know what we're going to say?"

"Leave it to me," Sue assured her. "I've got this."

Behind Sue's back, Ellen showed Tanya her crossed fingers. Tanya stifled a giggle.

"I can see you both in the reflection of this glass door," Sue said in a stern teacher voice. "Y'all should know by now that you can't get away with things like that around me. I'm smarter than you are."

Ellen and Tanya rolled their eyes.

"I saw that, too," Sue said just as an elderly, white woman opened the first door—the green, wooden door with the crucifix.

Through the glass door, the woman asked, "How can I help you?"

The woman was small with short, white hair, and she was wearing a breathing tube.

"Is this the Sisters of Mercy Convent?" Sue asked.

"Yes. What can I do for you ladies?"

"We're looking for Sister Anna Celeste. You see, my mother recently died, and in reading her diary, I discovered that she was a fan. Is the sister still alive, and if so, may we speak with her?"

Unable to believe that Sue had just lied to a nun, Ellen offered a polite smile and said nothing while she waited for the old woman to reply.

"I haven't heard that name in a long while," the woman said. "She was a dear, dear friend of mine, but I'm afraid she died some years back."

"Oh, that's too bad." Sue glanced back at her friends. "Would you mind telling us a bit about her, if you have a free moment?"

The old woman opened the glass door between them. "I'd love to. Why don't y'all come inside, and I'll put the kettle on."

They entered a simple front room with basic furnishings, and not the kind you could sink into with a good book and a cozy blanket. The walls were unadorned, except for another crucifix, a framed photo of the Virgin Mary, and a painting of the Last Supper.

"I'm Sister Thusala. Please make yourselves comfortable, and I'll be right back." The woman pushed an oxygen tank on a little blue cart toward what must have been the kitchen.

"Sister, that's not necessary," Ellen piped up. "We don't want to put you to any trouble. Why don't you sit with us for a few minutes, and we'll get out of your hair?"

"Alright, then." The nun smiled warmly at Ellen and took a seat in a wooden chair, allowing the three friends to take the orange sofa and pale blue armchair.

After introducing herself, her friends, and Moseby, Sue asked, "How did you first meet Sister Anna Celeste?"

Before Sister Thusala could reply, another woman—younger and black and wearing a simple blue dress and flats, entered the room with a bright smile on her face.

"I didn't know we had company, Sister Thusala."

"I wasn't expecting any, but here they are. Come over and meet them, Sister Bridget."

Sister Thusala made the introductions and then asked, "Would you mind bringing out my photo album? I'd like to show them a picture of Sister Anna Celeste."

"It would be my pleasure."

Sister Bridget left for a few moments and quickly returned, handing the album to Sue, who sat beside Ellen on the sofa. "I would stay and visit, but I must get to my class. It was nice to meet you all."

"Likewise," Ellen said.

Once the younger nun was gone, Sister Thusala said, "Sister Bridget teaches an adult literacy class on Saturday afternoons. We have two more sisters who live here with us. One of them runs an orphanage and the other ministers to the elderly at a nursing home. They won't be home until this evening."

"I hope we aren't taking up too much of your time by being here," Ellen said as Sue turned the pages of the photo album, which was rather sparse.

"There she is on the second page," the nun said, pointing. "I'm the short one, and she's the tall. That would have been taken in the late seventies, just a few months after I joined the Sisters of Mercy here in Biloxi."

"You were so young," Sue observed.

"It was the beginning of a marvelous life," the sister said with a smile. "And Sister Anna Celeste was my mentor. She showed me the ropes. Well, she was a mentor for a lot of people in Biloxi. She started the orphanage and a program for the poor. She was a wonderful servant of God who worked tirelessly for others. We were fortunate to have her for as long as we did."

Ellen leaned forward. "How did she die?"

"Peacefully in her sleep."

"That's the dream." Sue lifted her brows.

"She had a favorite joke she always told. She'd say, 'What do you call a nun in heaven?' And people would say, 'I don't know, Sister, a heaven nun? An angel nun?' And she'd say, 'Nun of the above.'"

The three friends chuckled.

"So that's what we call her around here, our 'Nun of the Above.'"

"That's sweet," Sue said as she turned the page of the photo album.

The one picture appeared to be the only photo the nun had of Sister Anna Celeste. Ellen supposed they didn't take many photos.

"Even though she was in her seventies, it was a surprise to all of us. We were devastated."

"I'm sorry," Tanya said. "That must have been hard. How long ago was it?"

"Let's see. It would have been in nineteen-eighty-seven—over thirty years ago."

Ellen met Tanya's look of surprise. Without saying anything, they knew what the other was thinking: *That's the same year the Sherrys were murdered.*

"I wish I could have known her," Sue said with a lamenting tone. "My mother wrote such beautiful words about her. She also wrote about a trip she'd made to Biloxi when Sister Anna Celeste introduced her to the infamous Vincent and Margaret Sherry."

"Such beautiful souls." Sister Thusala made the sign of the cross. "Biloxi continues to mourn their loss. You know, they used to bring us a meal at least once a month—usually from the Golden Corral, which is one of our favorites. It was such a thoughtful thing to do."

"When was the last time you saw them. Can you recall?" Sue asked.

"The day before they were killed," Sister Thusala said. "They brought us dinner on Monday night and stayed and ate with us. Nothing out of the ordinary happened. They had a belated birthday card for Sister Anna Celeste. It was a nice evening. We were shocked when we heard the news two days later."

Ellen and her friends exchanged curious glances. Had something been written on that birthday card that would shed some light on why the Sherrys were murdered? If the haunted planner wanted Ellen and her friends to see the Sherrys' appointment with

Sister Anna Celeste, it must be leading them to something important, right?

"And then Sister Anna Celeste died that same year?" Tanya asked.

"Exactly one week later," the nun replied.

Ellen tried to hide what she was thinking: *Was it possible that the person who had ordered the hit on the Sherrys had also been responsible for the nun's death?*

"Did Sister Anna Celeste leave a diary or letters behind that might have mentioned Sue's mother?" Ellen, struck with an idea, asked.

"She may have," Sister Thusala said, "but the only things I kept were her prayer book and rosary. Would you like to see them?"

"If it's no trouble," Sue said.

Disappointed not to have a box of letters to go through, Ellen barely gave the prayer book and rosary a second look as they were gingerly handed over by the elderly nun. But then, as Sue fingered through the gold-leaf pages, she and Ellen saw a folded piece of paper inconspicuously wedged inside.

Ellen was excited by the prospect of finding something and pretended to be overtaken by a coughing fit, asking the nun for a glass of water. While the sister was in the kitchen, Ellen and Sue quickly found the paper, plucked it from the prayer book, and unfolded it.

"What's that?" Tanya whispered, as she crossed the room to look over their shoulders.

"It's a letter from Margaret Sherry!" Sue whispered.

They could hear the nun returning, so Ellen quickly snatched the letter and tucked it into her purse before the nun emerged with her glass of water.

Coughing again, Ellen nodded, "Thank you, Sister." Then she drank down the water.

"Thank you so much for visiting with us," Sue said. "I guess we should let you get back to your day."

"It was my pleasure," Sister Thusala replied as they all headed for the door. "It's always nice to speak fondly of an old friend. I'm glad I could help."

Ellen couldn't get to the Honda Pilot fast enough.

"Let Sue drive away before you open it," Tanya insisted. "Sister Thusala might be watching from one of those windows."

Although Ellen thought Tanya was being overly cautious, she sat on her hands in the back seat with Moseby until they were back on Beach Boulevard, heading west toward their summer house. Then, she pulled the folded paper from her purse, opened it, and read:

"Dear Sister Anna Celeste,

Here is the key to the safety deposit box. Please wait at least six months before withdrawing from

the funds I've set aside for the expansion of your orphanage.

For extra security, please use this passcode when presenting the key: MQR554.

Yours in Christ,

Margaret Sherry."

"Oh, my gawd!" Sue cried from behind the wheel. "Do you think Margaret stole the money from Nix and gave it to Sister Anna Celeste?"

"Why else would she ask her to wait six months before making the withdrawal?" Tanya argued. "Besides, Vincent drove an old station wagon. I don't think they were wealthy enough to help with the expansion of the orphanage on their own."

"Maybe Vincent found out what Nix was up to and told his wife, and she convinced him to steal it from the crime ring and give it to the orphanage," Sue speculated.

Ellen read the letter again and again.

"Ellen?" Tanya asked. "What are you thinking?"

Ellen's heart pounded in her chest. "If Sister Anna Celeste died before she could access the money, is it still in the safety deposit box? Or did the Dixie Mafia find it?"

Tanya glanced back at Ellen. "I wonder what happened to the key?"

"Maybe the ghost of Angelique Fayard knows something," Ellen said, still feeling breathless. "She is the one who told us there was lost money."

"I wish we could have gotten a table at Mary Mahoney's tonight," Sue lamented.

Ellen leaned forward in the back seat as adrenaline coursed through her. "Why don't we go back to Old Biloxi Cemetery, to Peter Halat, Senior's grave, and try to contact her there?"

Ellen and her friends stopped in at the Visitors Center to use the restroom and purchase a bouquet of flowers from the gift shop. They hoped the flowers would make them less conspicuous while summoning a spirit at a grave.

Sue pulled the Honda Pilot into the cemetery from Beach Boulevard and followed the winding road to Pete Halat, Senior's obelisk headstone, where they all climbed out.

"Do you think the car's okay here?" Sue wondered as she closed the driver's door. "There's really no place to park."

Ellen lifted Mo from the back seat. "We can always move it if someone else comes along."

In the light of day, the cemetery was rather lovely. Huge oak trees shaded the hilly terrain that overlooked the gulf across the street. The traffic sounds were diminished by the sounds of waves washing in with the tide.

"This would be a beautiful place to rest in peace," Sue noted, as if she had read Ellen's mind.

Tanya laid the flowers at the base of the stone while Ellen dug through her purse for her pendulum. Moseby was happy to be out of his carrier, and he tugged on the end of his leash, wanting to explore.

"Not yet, Moseby-Mo," Ellen said sweetly. "Be good, and I'll take you for a walk in a minute."

"Do you want to use my homemade Ouija Board again?" Sue offered as she pulled a piece of paper from her purse.

"It worked last time," Tanya pointed out. "Let's try it."

Tanya took the paper and held it as she had in the attic of Mary Mahoney's, but the wind made it hard to keep both the paper and the pendulum steady.

"Why don't we try to capture EVPs instead?" Ellen suggested as she returned the pendulum to her purse and pulled out her EVP recorder.

"The wind might contaminate the evidence," Sue pointed out, "but I suppose we can give it a try."

"I'll start," Ellen offered.

As Ellen was about to call out to the spirit of Angelique Fayard, Moseby pulled again on his leash and wagged his tail at someone approaching. It was a tall, thin man with dark gray hair who appeared to be in his late seventies or early eighties.

The old man bent over and patted Moseby's head. "Hello."

Although the man had been talking to Mo, Ellen and her friends said, "Hello," back. Ellen quickly tucked her recorder into her purse.

The man wore a pair of blue jeans and a pale blue polo shirt and had a kind smile. "Did you know my father?"

Ellen tried to hide the look of shock that must have crossed her face as she glanced back at Sue and Tanya. Was this Pete Halat—the Pete Halat who was involved in the murders of Vincent and Margaret Sherry?

"Not really," Sue quickly said. "He was a friend of my mother. She died recently, and in her diary, she mentioned a pleasant trip to Biloxi and some of the friends she made while she was here. So, I'm going around and thanking them all for their kindness to her.

In fact, we just came from the Sisters of Mercy because Sister Anna Celeste was another friend she made here. Have you heard of her?"

Ellen wanted to sink into the ground and disappear. Was Sue really bringing up the woman to whom Margaret may have given the stolen money?

He surprised Ellen with a smile. "Everyone in Biloxi knew Sister Anna Celeste. She was an angel on earth."

"Did you know that she died exactly one week after Vincent and Margaret Sherry?" Sue asked.

Ellen bit her lip, and her knees felt suddenly wobbly. What was Sue's endgame?

"I did know that," he said with a frown. "That was a hard week for me and for all of Biloxi." Then he added, "And before you ask, I swear I had nothing to do with the Sherrys' deaths. I normally ignore people who bring it up, but out of respect for the friendship your mother had with my father, I'll give you the courtesy of hearing my side, if you want to hear it."

Ellen's brows nearly leapt from her forehead. So, this *was* Pete Halat, junior, and he wanted to tell his story. If Pete Halat, Senior had risen from his grave and had danced a jig, she wouldn't have been more shocked than she was in that moment.

"We would be grateful," Tanya said when both Sue and Ellen were too tongue-tied to offer a reply.

Pete knelt on the ground beside his father's grave and pet Moseby while the three women stood over him and listened. Although the old man was agile for his age, Ellen wondered if he would need help getting back to his feet.

"I'm sure you're familiar with the details of the Sherry murders, since you brought them up."

The three friends nodded.

"When I heard what Nix was up to with the homosexuals, I advised him to stop. I said this to him twice. Later, he paid our firm a large sum of money he'd earned in his scam hoping I could arrange a pardon. When that money came up missing and he accused me of stealing it, I was flabbergasted. I hadn't taken a dime and told him so to his face at Angola Prison. Hell, I'm the one who told him it was missing. Why would I do that if I stole it? He said if I hadn't taken it, who had? I said I didn't know and again denied that it was me. He later assumed it was Vince, probably because Vince would have been the only other authorized user on the account. I never would have put my best friend in harm's way. He and his wife were my dearest friends. It still breaks my heart that their children believed criminals like Bobby Joe Fabian and Mike Gillich over me."

Moseby, recognizing how distressed Pete was, licked the old man's chin.

"What a good boy," he said of the dog.

"Let me know if he's bothering you," Ellen said.

"Oh, he's not bothering me. I love dogs."

"Did you ever find out what happened to the money?" Sue asked.

Pete looked up at Sue and didn't bat an eye. "No."

Not sure whether she believed him but not wanting to take up too much more time from a man who had come to visit his father's grave, Ellen offered her hand to Pete. "It was nice meeting you. I'm sorry for your losses and for all the trouble life has put you through."

Ellen had another shock when Pete looked up at her with tears in his eyes. "I think that's the kindest thing anyone has said to me in a long time."

The three friends climbed back into the Pilot and left the old man alone with his thoughts and his truth and whatever words he had for his father.

CHAPTER ELEVEN

A Saturday Night Séance

Ellen was tired when Sue pulled into the driveaway of their summer house from Old Biloxi Cemetery. The German shepherd in the yard behind them looked tired, too. Or maybe he was depressed. Ellen wished she knew why the dog was always tethered to a stake in the front yard. Maybe she should knock on the door and find out.

But first, she needed a nap.

As they headed up to their second-floor unit, Sue asked, "Do y'all believe Pete's story?"

"He had no reason to lie to us," Tanya said. "I believe him."

"He seemed sincere," Ellen admitted. "But my brain is too tired to work it all out. I'm going to lie down."

Unsure how long she'd been asleep lying on top of the covers of the queen bed with Moseby, Ellen flinched awake to the sound of a loud thud overhead.

The book was at it again. Did it want to communicate something more to them?

A moment later, Tanya poked her head through the doorway of Ellen's room. "Did you hear that?"

Ellen sat up and rubbed her eyes. "Yes. Do you think it's trying to tell us something?"

Tanya shrugged. "Maybe. But after it hit me, I'm not sure I want to have anything more to do with it."

"I think it was the salt it was after, not you," Ellen pointed out.

"Even so."

Ellen climbed from the bed.

"Are you going to go up there?" Tanya asked.

"After I pee and get something to drink, yes. Maybe Sue will want to go."

From the hallway, Sue said, "I'm in."

Tanya groaned. "Fine. I'll go, too."

"Like there was ever any doubt," Sue teased.

Twenty minutes later, the three friends cautiously climbed the stairs to the third floor after having left Moseby safely in Ellen's room behind a closed door and a salted threshold. They carried their gear with them, planning to conduct a full investigation to get to the bottom of what was haunting Vincent Sherry's old planner and why.

They set up their full-spectrum cameras on tripods in three corners of the room. Ellen placed her EVP recorder on the bed beside the planner, which lay open on the bed to the month of the Sherry murders—September. Tanya lit three candles and set them on window ledges, and Sue, who had lit the end of a sage smudge stick, gave them each a bath with its smoke.

They placed a cat ball beside one of the candles and Mini Maglite flashlights beside the other two. The flashlights had been screwed to that interim place between on and off, so a spirit would have only to tap on it to communicate with them. Sue conducted some initial readings with the EMF detector while Tanya did the same with a thermometer. Ellen recorded their findings on her notepad using a headlamp strapped to her forehead to see by.

So far, the book was behaving itself.

"What do y'all want to try first?" Sue asked.

Ellen picked up her recorder and turned it on. "Let's ask questions with the EVP recorder. I'll go first . . . If there's anyone in here with us, anyone possessing this planner from 1987 that once belonged to Vincent Sherry, please know that we come in peace. We mean no harm. We want only to help. My name is Ellen. I'm a paranormal investigator. Can you tell me your name?"

They waited in silence for about fifteen to twenty seconds before Sue asked, "Can you tell us why you're here?"

The flame on one of the candles went out.

After another twenty seconds or so, Tanya asked, "Do you have a message for us?"

Ellen waited another thirty seconds and then turned off her recorder. "Now let's try using the spirit box app."

As she reached over to return her EVP recorder to the bed beside the book, the pages of the book began moving as if someone were quickly thumbing through them. The book moved toward Ellen's hand and seemed to bite her finger, giving her a paper cut.

"Ow!" she cried, shaking the finger that had been cut.

"What on earth?" Tanya cried. "Look!"

Drops of Ellen's blood had fallen on a lined but otherwise blank page of the planner and were moving across the page to spell, "Hello."

The three friends gaped as they watched the word form.

"Hello?" Sue said back to the book. "Can you tell us your name?"

They watched expectantly for a full minute before Sue turned to Ellen. "Try dropping more of your blood on the book. Maybe it needs something to use as ink."

One of the flashlights turned on.

"I think that means we're on the right track," Sue added.

"Why don't we use ink?" Tanya suggested. "Do you have a pen?"

Ellen pulled her pen from her purse and took it apart before drizzling some of the ink on the page.

Sue repeated, "Can you tell us your name?"

They watched anxiously for several minutes, but the ink was absorbed into the page as an ugly splotch.

"Maybe it has to be blood." Tanya bit a piece cuticle near her fingernail and squeezed a drop of her blood onto the planner.

The second flashlight turned on as the flame on the candle beside it was extinguished.

As soon as it hit the page, the blood moved and formed the words, "Mr. Mike."

Sue's brows disappeared beneath her bangs. "That was the nickname for Mike Gillich, the godfather of Biloxi!"

"Are you Mike Gillich?" Tanya asked before adding another drop of her blood to the page.

The blood formed the word, "Yes."

The three friends gasped.

"Oh, my gawd!" Sue cried. "This is incredible."

"What should we ask him next?" Tanya wondered.

"Where is the stolen mafia money," Ellen suggested.

Tanya had a hard time getting more blood from her bitten cuticle, so Ellen tried squeezing blood from her paper cut.

"Where is the stolen money?" Ellen asked as two drops of her blood hit the page.

They watched with amazement as the blood spelled, "Sister A C."

"Sister Anna Celeste?" Tanya wondered.

"But Sister Anna Celeste is dead," Sue pointed out. After biting off a piece of her cuticle, she added a drop of her blood to the page. "Do you know what she did with it?"

The blood formed the word, "No." Then more words formed, "She refused to tell me, so—"

"So what?" Sue asked.

When nothing more was written, Tanya said, "I think he needs more blood."

One of the flashlights turned off and back on.

Ellen squeezed another drop from her paper cut.

On the page, the blood formed the words, "I killed her."

All three women jumped back, putting more distance between themselves and the book.

With her heart beating against her ribs, Ellen panted and glanced at her friends. "I guess we know now how she died."

"I wonder how he made it look like she died peacefully in her sleep," Tanya whispered.

Sue took a few shaky steps back toward the book and, after biting off a little more of her cuticle, dropped blood onto the page as she asked, "Why are you here, possessing this book?"

The blood slowly formed the word, "Penance."

"Penance?" Sue repeated. "But how? How is being a crazy demon in a book a way of serving penance?"

She squeezed another drop of her blood onto the page, and the blood formed the words, "The truth will set me free."

Ellen glanced at her friends with wide eyes. "He wants to tell us what really happened."

"I think we're going to need more than a few drops of blood for that," Tanya whispered.

"I'll be right back." Ellen rushed from the third floor to the second-floor kitchen, where she took a filet knife from a drawer before heading upstairs again.

Once she was beside the bed between her friends, she held the knife to her palm over the book.

Tanya shuddered. "Are you sure about this?"

Ellen swallowed hard, her throat suddenly dry. Then, taking a deep breath, she made a cut in the palm of her left hand and squeezed a pool of her blood onto a second blank page.

"Tell us your truth," Ellen commanded.

The pool of blood began to swirl on the page like a magical snake.

"I want it known that I smothered the nun," was the first sentence made by the blood.

"What a horrible way to die," Tanya mumbled beneath her breath.

Next, the blood spelled out, "And Nix tricked me."

"Tricked you?' Ellen read aloud. "How?"

"Pete would pay, too," the blood wrote on one line, "I thought he meant that Pete was in on the hitman."

Ellen glanced at her friends. "Pete Halat?"

The blood formed the word, "Yes."

"So, Nix lied to you?" Sue asked.

"No," the blood wrote. "By pay, he meant Pete would suffer. I didn't learn the truth until—"

"Until what?" Tanya asked.

They waited, but nothing more was written.

"He needs more blood," Sue inferred.

Ellen attempted to squeeze more from her palm. The blood had already begun to dry, and the wound was tender to the touch, but she was able to squeeze another few drops onto the next page.

"After my death," the blood wrote.

Tanya covered her mouth. "That's so sad."

"Oh, gosh," Ellen murmured.

"Give me that," Sue said of the knife. Then, after cutting across her palm, she, too, filled a new page with her blood while asking, "Do you have anything more to say?"

"Let the truth be known," the blood wrote.

"But why would anyone believe us?" Ellen asked. "No one will believe that Mike Gillich confessed from beyond the grave. Even if we show our video coverage, they'll think it was a trick."

"Pressure Nix to tell the truth," the blood wrote. "He knows about the nun, too. Tell him I said peanut butter with pickles is good. Tell him he'll want to confess before he dies. It'll be torture otherwise. Get my daughter Trina's help."

Ellen sucked in her lips. This was powerful stuff, and she didn't know what to make of it. As much as she wanted to help this troubled soul make peace, she couldn't imagine going to a prison and getting an infamous crime leader to confess anything, even with the help of Gillich's daughter. Why would Trina believe her, anyway?

"Do you have anything else to say?" Sue asked as she drizzled a little more of her blood onto the book.

The blood swirled into the words, "I'm so sorry and full of regret. It torments me."

Tanya took out her phone. "When did Mike Gillich die? Oh, here it is. He died in 2012 of cancer."

"So, he's been tormented by this for over ten years," Sue remarked.

"And that's on top of the nine years he spent in prison," Tanya said.

Sue cocked her head to the side. "Though, some may feel he hasn't suffered long enough."

"That's not for us to decide," Ellen argued. "We've made it our policy to help every ghost we come across to find peace. Right? And getting the truth out will help others, too, like Pete and his family and the Sherrys' children. And it might even help Nix if he rights this wrong before he dies. We're about peace, not punishment. We're about righting wrongs. We're about setting people free without judgment."

"Everybody deserves a chance to be redeemed," Tanya agreed.

"Amen, sisters," Sue said. "He paid his time. We can't refuse a soul in need."

Tanya frowned. "It won't be easy getting Nix to confess. But I'm willing to try. Just don't hit me with that book again."

Ellen chuckled at Tanya, even though her friend hadn't meant to make a joke. It tickled her funny bone, and she couldn't stop.

Her friends started laughing, too, perhaps to relieve their nervousness and anxiety. It felt good to laugh after so much seriousness and sorrow. Sue shrieked and held her belly. Tanya covered her mouth, her face red with laughter. Ellen shook her head, unable to stop.

"Oh, no!" Ellen cried. "I think I peed again!"

CHAPTER TWELVE

The Golden Key

Ellen and her friends spent Sunday morning composing an email to send to Mike Gillich's daughter on her law firm's website. After a lot of starts and stops and revisions, this is what they came up with:

Dear Trina Gillich,

We've come across new information regarding the Shery Murders that implicates your father and exonerates Pete Halat. We're only in town for a few days and would like to arrange a meeting with you as soon as possible. You can reach us at this number.

Ellen added their names and her phone number and hit send, hoping for the best, before she and her friends headed to the Port City Café for breakfast, followed by a tour of the Beauvoir.

Unlike the Visitors Center across from the lighthouse, the Beauvoir consisted of a single story. It was raised off the ground several feet, designed that way by its original builder so that the breezes could flow beneath the house and keep it cool. According to a pamphlet Ellen had picked up from a gift shop in the new and gorgeous

Jefferson Davis Library, the design is what saved the Beauvoir from utter destruction during storm surges.

The pamphlet went on to explain that the house was built by a Madison County planter who used it as a summer house, as the soil was not suitable for planting. The house was eventually purchased by a woman who was a friend of Jefferson Davis. Sarah Ann Dorsey named the estate Beauvoir because of its beautiful view. When Jefferson Davis was looking for a place to write his memoirs, Dorsey invited him to stay with her. Dorsey later died of cancer. She had willed her home to Davis.

Sometime after Davis's death, the house was sold to the to the United Confederate Veterans. Two conditions of the sale were, first, that the property was used as a home for Confederate veterans, their wives or widows, and their servants; and second, that the property be a memorial to Jefferson Davis in perpetuity. The house operated at a home for Confederates from 1903 to 1957. According to the pamphlet, more than 2,000 veterans, wives, widows, and servants lived in the home and 771 of them are buried in the Beauvoir cemetery.

Although the exterior of the house reminded Ellen of the design of the Visitors Center with its central flight of steps leading to a high, wrap-around porch, tall columns, and symmetrical windows, the interior was simpler and more authentic looking, with the main hall in the center of the home serving as a parlor and dining area and smaller rooms off the hall serving as bedrooms and a library. Original paintings and artifacts, some damaged by the ravages of past hurricanes, were prominently displayed, and a discoloration on the interior walls marked the four-foot water line caused by Hurricane Katrina when the house was flooded.

From the home tour, Ellen and her friends walked along the garden and the cemetery and the lovely surrounding views.

"I feel sick," Tanya whispered. "I think by purchasing my ticket, I inadvertently supported an ideology I despise."

"What makes you think this place espouses any kind of ideology?" Sue asked, keeping her voice down so as not to be overheard by other tourists.

"I saw a book in the gift shop, where we picked up our tickets," Tanya said. "It was called *The Little Sambo.*"

Ellen covered her mouth. "Why didn't you say?"

"Wait, I don't understand," Sue said. "Why would that bother you?"

Ellen and Tanya were taken aback.

"Just Google it," Tanya suggested as they continued their walk along the garden.

Before they could further discuss the book that Tanya and Ellen had found so offensive, Ellen's cell phone rang. It was a Mississippi number. Thinking it might be Trina Gillich, Ellen answered it.

"Hello?" Ellen said into the phone.

"Is this Ellen McManius?" a woman asked.

"Yes," Ellen replied.

"This is Sandra from the law office of Trina Gillich calling in response to your email."

"Oh, yes. Thank you for getting back to me."

"Would you be available to come in tomorrow morning at ten o'clock to speak with Ms. Gillich?"

"Yes," Ellen said. "Ten o'clock works just fine."

"Wonderful. We'll see you then."

Ellen hung up the phone. "We have an appointment with Trina Gillich tomorrow at ten."

Tanya shook her head. "I sure hope we know what we're doing."

"You and me both, sister," Sue agreed.

Sunday evening, Ellen and her friends headed to Mary Mahoney's Old French House for their seven o'clock reservation eager for an opportunity to speak again in the attic with Angela Fayard about the missing mafia money. After parking, they walked through a front courtyard and into a building that was once a mall, following the corridor to the restaurant entrance. Along the walls of the corridor were framed photos of Mary Mahoney and her family, along with photos of famous people who had dined there. Ellen recognized a photo of Denzel Washington and another of the actor who played Gibbs from *NCIS*. There was an article about John Grisham having referred to the restaurant in two of his books. As Ellen scanned a few more of the photos, she had a shock.

"Look!" she cried to her friends. "It's Sister Anna Celeste! And look what she's wearing around her neck!"

Moseby, reacting to her excitement, licked her chin from his cloth pooch carrier.

"That can't be *the* key," Sue said. "She would have only had it for a week before she passed away."

"I wonder when that picture was taken," Tanya said. "She looks like she's in her seventies. Wasn't she in her seventies when she died?"

"I believe so," Ellen said. "What if that *is* the key? Let's ask Bob when the photo was taken and if he knows anything about her necklace."

Unlike their first visit when they dined in the courtyard, they were seated indoors in a small room that had three other tables. The room was beautifully decorated with a crystal chandelier, sweeping swag valances of silk and beads, picture rails trimmed in white beadboard, and a fireplace with a painting of Renaissance-period mother, father, and baby on its mantle stretching all the way to the high ceiling. Ellen and her friends were seated at a white-linen table for three beside the fireplace.

"I love how intimate this feels," Tanya whispered.

"Me, too," Sue agreed.

Ellen glanced at her menu. "I think I want the same thing I had last time. It was so delicious."

"What did you have last time?" Tanya asked.

"The Queen Ixolib." They'd been told by their waiter during their previous visit that Ixolib was Biloxi spelled backwards. "The fish stuffed with crab and white sauce over pasta. Oh, my gosh, was it good."

After their waiter took their order, Ellen asked him if Bob had time to come to their table. The waiter said he would let the owner know.

"I'm sure he'll make it by to see you before you've finished your meal. I'll go put your order in now."

"So, what are we going to say to Trina Gillich tomorrow?" Sue asked after their waiter had left. "We need to get our story straight."

"Well," Ellen began, "I can tell you what we *won't* say. We won't say that the ghost of your father is haunting the lost planner that once belonged to Vincent Sherry."

"No," Tanya agreed. "We won't say *that*."

Before they could plan out what they *would* say, Bob appeared beside their table.

"Hello, ladies. Welcome back."

"Hey, Bob," Sue said with a smile. "You're looking spiffy tonight. I should take a photo with you to send to my husband to make him jealous."

Ellen felt the blood rushing to her cheeks. Was Sue serious?

"Let's do it, little lady," Bob said. "Who wants to snap the photo?"

Tanya took out her phone. "I'll take it."

Bob put an arm around Sue and smiled as Tanya took the picture.

"Got it," Tanya said.

"Thank you, Bob," Sue said with a demure smile.

Was she really flirting with him?

"My pleasure," he said.

"Speaking of photos," Ellen began. "We noticed a photo of you and Sister Anna Celeste in the corridor on the way over."

"Oh, yes. Sister Anna Celeste was my mentor. She was like a second mother to me—God rest her soul."

"When was that photo taken?" Tanya asked.

"Two days before she passed. Her cat had died, and she needed my help. I had no idea it would be the last time I'd ever see her alive. She was a good woman. One of the best. Biloxi owes a lot to her. She used to tell a joke, 'What do you call a nun in heaven?'"

"Nun of the Above," Sue said with a grin.

"That's right! You know that one, then."

"Say, Bob?" Ellen began. "Do you know what happened to the necklace she was wearing in that photo? I'm just curious."

"That's the one with the key, right? She was buried in it. I remember that last day I saw her, I asked her about it because I hadn't never seen it before, and she said it was a gift from a generous soul, so we thought it only fitting that she should be buried with it."

Bob spent a few more minutes with them telling his jokes, but Ellen was only half listening. Her mind was churning with one thought: How on earth could they get Sister Anna Celeste's body exhumed? There was no way she was going to try digging it up in the dark of night. She and Tanya had dug up too many graves as it was. Besides, her palm was still sore from where she'd cut it. But they had to think of a way to get the nun exhumed. It was their only chance of finding the lost money.

Once they had finished their delicious meal, Ellen and her friends paid their bill and then, giddy with excitement, snuck up the attic stairs with hopes of contacting Angelique Fayard again. However, when they reached the top of the staircase, they found the room illuminated and the tables occupied by diners.

"What?" Sue asked with surprise.

"Oh, no," Tanya muttered.

"Can I help you, ladies?" a passing waitress asked.

"We're looking for the restroom," Ellen quickly said.

"It's downstairs," the waitress replied. "Would you like to follow me?"

Disappointed, Ellen and her friends followed the waitress downstairs to the restroom. Left alone outside the ladies' room door, Ellen asked her friends, "Now what should we do?"

Tanya pushed open the door. "We may as well go since we're right here."

"Let's come back tonight," Sue suggested as she followed Tanya into the restroom. "It doesn't have to be the attic. We can summon her from the courtyard, if it's open, or even the parking lot."

Ellen frowned. "I guess that's better than nothing."

"And if that doesn't work," Tanya said from inside a stall. "We can try the lighthouse and the cemetery."

Not needing to use the facilities, Ellen waited for her friends by the sink. She had a shock when suddenly the reflection looking back at her was not her own. The woman had brown hair pinned high on her head, and she was wearing a Victorian-style dress.

Ellen gasped. Was this Angelique Fayard?

The woman put a finger to her lips just as Ellen had been about to ask. The hot water turned on, and steam filled the air between them. Then, on the mirror over the sink, words were written in the condensation: IN THE GROUND.

Ellen gawked as she tried to process what she'd just seen. A ghost had appeared in the mirror and had left her a message.

Once she'd come to terms with what was happening, Ellen whispered, "We know. Bob told us. The key is in the ground, buried with Sister Anna Celeste."

Tanya emerged from her stall. "Who are you talking to?"

With wide eyes, Ellen pointed a shaky finger at the mirror. Although Angelique's image had disappeared, the words IN THE GROUND had remained behind.

"What's going on out there?" Sue asked from her stall.

"We had a visitor," Ellen replied.

Sue finished up and joined them at the sink to wash her hands. "Are you sure you didn't write that, Ellen?"

"Look at her," Tanya said. "She's shaking like a leaf."

"I didn't write it," Ellen insisted. "I think Angelique wants us to find that key."

Sue dried her hands before tossing the paper towel into the trash. "Maybe Trina Gillich can help us with that, too."

"How do you propose we do that?" Tanya wanted to know.

"I got skills, girlfriend."

CHAPTER THIRTEEN

Mr. Mike

Sunday night, the three friends enjoyed the view in wooden rockers on their balcony of the waxing gibbous moon and stars sparkling on the dark waters of the gulf, the lulling sounds of their ebb and flow audible over the occasional sounds of traffic on Beach Boulevard. Ellen had been continually surprised by the small-town atmosphere in Biloxi. It was teeming with tourists, but you wouldn't know it by the traffic.

"This margarita is delicious," Tanya said to Sue, who sat in the middle rocker between her and Ellen.

"Good. Glad you like it. There's more in the freezer when you're ready."

"Oh, this is plenty." Then, Tanya added, "I still can't believe you were flirting with Bob Mahoney."

Sue chuckled. "Just making sure I still got it."

"You got something, that's for sure," Tanya teased. "Maybe early onset."

"Well, if Tom is having an affair, let's hope so," Sue joked.

Tanya waved a hand through the air. "Tom is not having an affair."

Sue turned to Ellen. "You okay? You've been quiet."

Although Mo's presence on Ellen's lap was comforting, she rocked in the chair with an anxious heart. "We need a game plan, ladies."

Sue nodded. "I've already got one figured out."

Ellen looked up at her. "You do? Spill."

"We'll tell Trina *we* discovered the planner. We don't want to involve Brenda and John against their will."

"But how will we explain why we were on the third floor?" Tanya asked.

Ellen snapped her fingers. "We'll say we were looking for Moseby. He was lost, and we found him hiding in there, which is the truth."

Sue took a sip of her marg. "Okay, good. And while we were looking for Moseby, I tripped and fell, and some floorboards came loose, and there it was."

Ellen lifted her brows. "Yes. That sounds good."

"I wonder how the planner ended up here," Tanya mused.

"Why don't we ask it?" Sue suggested.

A half hour later, after they'd finished their margaritas, Ellen secured Moseby in her bedroom with another chicken-flavored treat and then followed her friends with their gear to the third floor, hoping to talk again with the ghost of Mike Gillich.

Although it was less unsettling on the third floor now that they knew the identity of the ghost, the fact that he'd been the godfather of Biloxi and had been responsible for the deaths of at least three people created another kind of intensity and oppression in the air. The cobwebs, thick dust, lack of electricity, and loose floorboards didn't help, either.

As they entered the bedroom where the book lay open on the bed, Ellen, wearing a headlamp to see by, said, "We come in peace."

They set up their cameras, Mini Maglite flashlights, and candles. They'd also brought up the EMF generator hoping the ghost could draw energy from it instead of their blood. Their fingers were sore and scabbed over, as were Ellen and Sue's left palms.

Ellen laid the Ouija Board and planchette on top of the largest box. Then they gathered around it—Sue and Ellen on the edge of the bed and Tanya across from them on her knees—before gently touching their fingertips to the planchette.

"Ready?" Sue asked.

Ellen and Tanya nodded.

Sue moved the planchette around the board in a circular motion. "We only wish to speak with Mike Gillich, Jr., also known as Mr. Mike and the godfather of Biloxi. No one else may speak with us. No entities may attach to or attempt to possess us. We have come in peace to help the tormented spirit of Mike Gillich." Sue took a deep breath and centered the planchette on the board. "Mike Gillich, we would like to use this board to communicate with you. You can move the planchette to *yes*," she moved it to *yes*, "or over here to *no*," she moved it to *no*, "and use these letters and numbers to make words and sentences." She moved the planchette to the center again. "Why don't we start with an easy one. Mike Gillich, are you here?"

The flames on all three candles began to dance wildly. The headlight strapped to Ellen's forehead blinked off and on. One of the flashlights turned on, too, before turning off again. But the planchette did not move.

"Mike Gillich, is that you?" Sue asked. "If you are here with us, please move this planchette to *yes*."

"Ahhh!" Tanya jumped to her feet and backed up to the door of the room.

"What's wrong?" Ellen asked.

"I heard a whisper in my ear," she said with a shudder. "I heard *yes* right by my ear."

"I hope the cameras caught it," Sue said.

"Why? Don't you believe me?"

"Of course, I do. It would just be nice to have it on camera. That's all I meant."

"Come back, Tanya, and let's try again," Ellen suggested. "Let's see if we can get him to use this planchette."

Tanya returned to her place on her knees by the box and placed her fingertips on the planchette.

"Mike Gillich?" Sue called. "If you want to whisper in someone's ear, you can whisper in mine, but Tanya doesn't like it."

"I just wasn't expecting it, that's all."

"But we'd prefer you to use this planchette and board to communicate with us," Ellen added.

"Just to confirm that you are here, Mike," Sue began, "will you push this planchette to *yes*?"

Slowly, the planchette began to move. After a few seconds, it stopped on yes.

"Thank you so much, Mike." Sue recentered the planchette on the board. "Or, maybe I should call you Mr. Mike. Can you also confirm that you were responsible for the deaths of Vincent and Margaret Sherry and Sister Anna Celeste?"

Less slowly this time, the planchette moved to *yes*.

"And can you confirm that Pete Halat had nothing to do with their murders?" Sue asked as she recentered the planchette again.

The planchette moved to *yes*.

"Did Pete have anything to do with the Lonely Hearts Scam?" Ellen asked.

The planchette moved in a circle and stopped between *yes* and *no*.

"What do you think that means?" Tanya wondered. "Maybe Mike doesn't know."

"Or, maybe Pete wasn't in on the scam but knew about it and didn't do anything to prevent it," Ellen speculated.

The planchette moved to *yes*.

"Thank you, Mr. Mike." Sue recentered the planchette. "Can you also confirm that you believe Sister Anna Celeste knew where the stolen money from the Lonely Hearts Scam was located?"

One of the flashlights flashed on and off again as the planchette moved to *yes*.

"And do you know where the money is?" Sue asked.

The planchette moved to *no*.

"We will ask your daughter to arrange a meeting with Nix," Ellen said, "but is there anything we can say to her in case she doesn't want to help us? Is there a special code word or message from you that will let her know it came from you?"

The planchette moved to the letter T.

"T," Tanya said.

Then the planchette moved to W-E-E-T-Y.

"Wait, Tweety?" Tanya asked.

The planchette moved to *yes*. Then it continued to B-I-R-D.

Sue nodded. "Oh, Tweety Bird. Is that what you called your daughter, Trina?"

The planchette moved to *yes*.

Tanya leaned over the box and asked Ellen, "I thought we weren't going to tell the daughter about her father's ghost."

"Not unless we have no choice," Ellen said.

"It's good to have options," Sue agreed.

"Mr. Mike?" Tanya began. "How did Vincent Sherry's planner end up here? Did you put it here?"

The planchette moved to *yes*.

"When?" Ellen asked.

The planchette spelled out 1-9-8-7.

"Right after the murders," Sue concluded.

The planchette moved to *yes*. Then, it continued to spell out M-Y.

"My," Sue read when the planchette paused.

The planchette spelled out H-O-U-S-E.

"This was your house?" Ellen asked.

The planchette moved to *yes*. Then, it continued to H-I-D-I-T-I-N-A-T-T-I-C.

"He hid it in the attic," Sue said.

The planchette moved to *yes*.

"How did you come to haunt the planner?" Tanya asked.

The planchette spelled out P-U-N-I-S-H-M-E-N-T.

The three friends looked at one another with wide eyes. Hade Mike Gillich been condemned by God or some other heavenly authority to possess the planner?

The flames on the candles began to dance wildly again.

"Is there anything else you want us to tell your daughter?" Sue asked.

The planchette spelled out S-O-R-R-Y.

"I wonder if Mike Gillich can finally move on and find peace," Ellen said. "Should we say a prayer for him?"

The ladies bowed their heads as Ellen prayed, "We ask God to forgive the transgressions of Mike Gillich and accept him into your heavenly kingdom. We pray that Mike is truly sorry for his crimes and that, if he is, he will find a way to forgive himself and find peace. Mike, look for the light and for the warmth of your loved ones who have passed and seek your everlasting peace."

The flames on the candles went out at once, as did Ellen's headlamp, leaving them with nothing to see by but the moon and starlight coming in through the windows.

CHAPTER FOURTEEN

Mr. Mike's Daughter

Ellen sat in a wooden chair between her friends across the table from an attractive woman in her late sixties with shoulder-length blonde hair, bright blue eyes, and perfectly white teeth. Ellen pressed her lips together to cover her own teeth as she wondered what this woman's secret was to maintaining such a lovely complexion and smile.

"We know this is a bit unorthodox." Sue admitted.

Trina Gillich pushed her long, blonde bangs from her eyes and laughed. "That's an understatement, but let's hear it. What have you got?"

Ellen leaned forward. "We were told that your father misunderstood Kirksey Nix when Nix said that Pete Halat would pay. Your father thought he meant that Pete would help pay for the hitman they would hire to kill the Sherrys."

"But Nix just meant that Pete would suffer," Sue clarified.

Ellen nodded. "Nix failed to correct your father when he testified that Pete was in on it."

Trina Gillich, still smiling with incredulity, lifted her chin. "I'm going to need you to reveal your source."

Tanya glanced at each of her friends before asking, "Why? If we can get Nix to corroborate what our source said, why do you need his name?"

The attorney stood up from her chair and sat on the corner of her desk, the other corner of which was covered with framed photos of friends and family. "I can't set up a meeting with Nix unless your source checks out."

Sue lifted a finger. "We'll tell you in a moment, but we'd rather tell you what else we learned and reveal the source after."

"Fine. I'm listening."

"Your father believed that Sister Anna Celeste had been given the stolen money by the Sherrys to expand an orphanage, and we have other evidence to support that." Ellen pulled out the note that had been wedged in Sister Anna Celeste's prayer book and told Trina where it had been found.

Tanya crossed one leg over the other with a nervous restlessness. "The sister was wearing a key in a photo taken with Bob Mahoney of Mary Mahoney's Old French House—"

"I know who Bob Mahoney is."

Tanya's face reddened. "Sorry. Anyway, Bob said the nun was buried with the key still around her neck."

"So," Sue continued, "we were hoping that, in addition to arranging a meeting with Nix, you could get a court order to have Sister Anna Celeste exhumed."

Trina Gillich laughed again—for many seconds this time. "I'm going to need more evidence than this note—that may or may not have been written by Margaret Sherry."

"What about this?" Sue handed over Vincent Sherry's 1987 planner.

Trina took the book and thumbed through it as her jaw dropped open. "Where did you get this?"

Sue told their made-up story about chasing Moseby up to the third floor of their summer house rental on Beach Boulevard.

"What address?" Trina wanted to know.

Tanya lifted her brows. "Ten twenty-two."

Trina carried the planner behind her desk and returned to her chair, her face somber now. "That was my childhood home. We moved out after Daddy was incarcerated."

Ellen glanced at her friends but made no comment. The wheels inside Trina's head seemed to be turning.

"That house had meant the world to him," she added after a moment. "In fact, we rented the place out for him so he could live there for the last two years of his life. He lived there until he died of cancer in 2012."

"I'm sorry for your loss," Sue said just as Ellen was about to say the same.

"We were so thankful he didn't have to spend his final years in prison. We were glad to have ten really good years with him before the cancer set in. We were with him when he died—all of us, even his beloved dog, Rocky. The dog was so depressed after Daddy died, that he went, too, just a few days after."

Ellen wondered if Trina ever thought about the children of Vincent and Margaret Sherry. They would have liked more time with their parents, too.

They gave the attorney a few minutes to reflect, and then Ellen said, "If you turn to September, you'll see that Sister Anna Celeste was one of the last people to see the Sherrys alive."

Sue added, "Bob Mahoney told us she was buried with the key. Can you get a court order to exhume her body? It might be the only way to find the stolen mafia money."

At the mention of the money, Trina's eyes shot up at Sue. "Have you told anyone else about the money?"

The three friends shook their heads.

"Good. Let's keep this confidential. We wouldn't want a media circus over nothing."

"But what will you tell the judge?" Sue asked.

"I'll tell the judge, of course, but I wouldn't want this information falling into the wrong hands."

The three friends nodded.

"Right," Sue agreed. "Does this mean you'll do it?"

Trina laid the planner on her desk and looked each one of them in the eye. "First, I'm going to need the name of your source."

Ellen glanced at her friends. They'd agreed that she'd be the one to explain, since she had a better understanding of what it was like to be a skeptic. "This will be hard to believe, so brace yourself."

"Go on."

"We're paranormal investigators," Ellen continued. "We spoke with a spirit who was haunting that planner."

The attorney's blue eyes widened.

"He claimed to be your father," Ellen said.

The attorney's mouth dropped open.

"He told us he used to call you Tweety Bird," Ellen said. "I'm so sorry if this is upsetting to you. We aren't trying to trick you, or to manipulate you, or to do anything underhanded. We know not everyone believes, but—"

"I believe you," the woman said, her eyes wide and welled with tears. "I'm a very spiritual person. My father was, too. I believe you, and I want to talk to him."

Sue frowned. "That may not be possible, I'm afraid."

"Why not?" Trina Gillich demanded.

Tanya leaned forward. "You see, he was suffering—tormented by his past. He wanted the truth out, so he could find peace."

"We prayed over him and helped him move on," Ellen explained.

"Can't we try anyway?" Tears were now spilling from the woman's eyes. "Please?"

"Of course," Sue said. "We'll be there a few more days yet. When would you like to come by?"

Trina Gillich stood up from behind her desk. "Now."

In her silver Porsche, Trina Gillich followed Ellen and her friends to the summer house on Beach Boulevard.

"I hope she's not going to be too devastated," Ellen said from the back seat of the Pilot on the way over.

"Maybe we'll get lucky," Sue said. "We need to think positive thoughts."

When they pulled into the driveaway, Ellen was surprised and relieved to see that the German shepherd was no longer tethered to the front porch. Finally, she thought. Maybe the arrangement in the yard had only been temporary. Maybe the dog had been sprayed by a skunk or had ringworm or something that had prevented the family from keeping him indoors.

Trina Gillich followed the three friends upstairs to their second-floor unit, where Ellen checked on Moseby, whom she'd left with a treat in her room.

"Just a little while longer, Moseby-Mo," she said to him before closing the door again.

"I have such fond memories of this place," Trina said as she crossed the main living room to the front balcony.

"You want to take a look around?" Tanya offered.

Trina turned away from the balcony doors. "No. I want to talk to my father."

"Please, don't get your hopes up," Sue warned. "I'd hate to see you disappointed. Maybe you can find comfort in knowing that he's finally at peace."

"Let's just give it a try, shall we? Lead the way."

Ellen led the way up the stairs to the third floor. When she opened the door, the air was noticeably different. Despite the thick dust and the cobwebs, the air felt lighter.

"My bedroom was up here," Trina said mournfully. "What a mess. The landlord kept this floor locked and off limits while my father was renting, so this is the first time I'm seeing it since we moved out."

Ellen had a feeling that Brenda and John would be renovating the upstairs soon enough.

"Your father's ghost was through here," Sue said, leading the way through the bath and its adjacent room."

"This was my brother's room," Trina said through quivering lips. "What a blast from the past." She walked past the cardboard boxes still strewn on the floor to the closet. "I used to hide in there, hoping to scare him. Wait, is there something in there?"

Trina took several steps back as the German shepherd from the yard behind the house stepped forward.

"Rocky?" Tanya said, her voice a whole octave higher. "Rocky, is that you?"

The dog wagged its tail and pranced toward her with a happy yelp. Trina backed up and fell to her bottom near a window, knocking over one of the boxes as she laughed and embraced the dog.

Everyone in the room was stunned when Trina's arms moved through the dog. He was an apparition and not a corporal being, as Ellen had originally believed.

"What on earth?" Tanya whispered.

Ellen gawked at the vision, wondering how on earth it had been tethered in the neighbor's yard for so many days. Had Rocky's soul been waiting on his master's?

Just then, another apparition appeared in front of the window. The old man was barely visible in the late morning sunlight streaming into the room.

"There you are, Rocky," the specter said. "Come on. It's time to go."

Trina hadn't moved from the floor. Her eyes and mouth were opened wide. "Daddy?"

The apparition noticed her for the first time. He studied her for a few seconds before saying, "Tweety Bird? Is that you?"

Trina jumped to her feet and ran to embrace her father, but just as she reached him, he and the dog vanished.

"Daddy!" she cried. "Come back! I want to talk to you!"

Ellen and her friends watched silently for several painful minutes as the daughter cried out with desperate tears for her father to return.

Finally, Sue put a hand on Trina's shoulder. "I think he's resting now. Why don't we go downstairs? I have a margarita with your name on it."

"Thank you, but I think I need to be alone. Y'all saw that, right? I didn't imagine it?"

"We saw," Ellen assured her. "You didn't imagine it."

"We're glad you got to see him one more time," Tanya added.

Tears fell from Trina's eyes as she nodded. "Me, too. Thank you."

Ellen was shocked when the attorney gave each of them a hug, repeating, "Thank you."

As they followed her downstairs, Trina said, "I'll get to work on those two requests and get back with you as soon as I know something."

CHAPTER FIFTEEN

The Biloxi Orphanage

After a delicious lunch at McElroy's, Ellen and her friends paid a visit to the Sisters of Mercy Orphanage in Biloxi to see the organization that Sister Anna Celeste had founded and the one for which Margaret Sherry gave her life in an attempt to support and expand it.

Located just two blocks away from the Sisters of Mercy Convent, the orphanage was not what Ellen had expected an orphanage to be. It was a block of old houses rather than a single dormitory-style building. The backs of the homes had been transformed into the fronts, and what was once a series of backyards had become a common area without fencing. Seven houses faced each other, and in the center was a park with swings, picnic tables, a basketball court, and a small, above-ground swimming pool.

The administrative offices were located inside one of the houses. It, like the others, looked like your run-of-the-mill ranch-style home, not unlike the Sisters of Mercy Convent. With Moseby in his cloth pooch carrier, Ellen followed Sue and Tanya inside to meet with the director, Sister Martha.

Sister Martha appeared to be in her late thirties with black, curly, shoulder-length hair, green eyes, and a thin physique. Nearly as tall as Tanya, she was mostly legs and neck. After introductions, Sister Martha welcomed them and offered to give them a tour but first wanted to show them the model in her office.

"This is our dream for the future of this organization," the sister explained. "It's modeled after the Palmer House, which was founded in Columbus, Mississippi in the eighteen hundreds. Later, in 1960, Palmer House changed its design to what they call the cottage style. Rather than housing children in one big building, they grouped them into smaller homes, all on the same campus, with a house mother and a house father in each home, to make their experiences more like a typical family life."

"What a wonderful concept," Tanya remarked.

"It really is," Sister Martha agreed. "Especially when we get siblings. We try our very best to keep them together in the same cottage."

"Where do the children go to school?" Sue asked.

"The Biloxi public schools," the nun replied. "Just like the other kids, a bus picks them up in the mornings and drops them off in the afternoons. Of course, they're off for the summer, so we must keep them occupied as best we can."

Ellen nodded. "I love that they aren't isolated from the rest of society."

"We're hoping those days are behind us," Sister Martha said. "When the children are in school, they eat free breakfasts and lunches provided by the schools. House parents cook their dinners in their cottages, just like a regular family. During the summer, we try to make it easier on the house parents by having community lunches. This administration building has a common area with enough tables and chairs to accommodate everyone. We have a big-screen movie projector in there, too, and often have movie nights to help occupy the kids in the summers."

"What will it take for you to reach this dream of the future?" Sue wondered.

The nun frowned. "Time and a lot of resources. We're currently overcrowded. The homes should only have six to eight children living in them with two house parents, but they each have ten and one has eleven."

"Ten and eleven children to a house?" Tanya repeated. "How many bedrooms?"

"Some have three and others four, so we have three kids to a room. It's not horrible. The kids on *The Brady Bunch* did it, right?"

"If the kids have the bedrooms, where do the house parents sleep?" Ellen wondered.

"Each living room has a sofa bed," Sister Martha explained. "Would you like to see one of the cottages?"

"Sure," Ellen replied.

As they stepped out of the administrative building, they followed a sidewalk around the park, where a group of teenagers were playing basketball.

"We want to acquire the properties on the other side of these cottages here as they become available," the sister pointed to the right, "but we can't afford them yet. Eventually, we'd like to build or convert existing properties into another campus, because we're limited in how far we can expand in this area."

"So, you currently have sixty-one children living in six houses?" Sue asked.

"Yes." Sister Martha led them past the above-ground pool where ten children—six girls and four boys ranging in age from five or six to fifteen or sixteen—were playing while two adults watched on. "The cottages rotate pool privileges. Each house gets a different day of the week, and no one swims on Sundays, so the pool can be cleaned and the families can attend mass."

"Are these children waiting to be adopted?" Tanya asked.

"Some are. Others are social orphans who are here because their biological parents can't take care of them. The parents might be in rehab or prison or experiencing some other temporary hardship. Some of those children might return to their parents one day."

"How long, on average, does each child remain here?" Ellen asked.

"It varies wildly from one case to another. Some live the bulk of their childhoods here. That's why it's so important that we provide as much support as we can. We're currently trying to expand our mental health services."

"I'm glad to hear that's a priority," Tanya commented. "I'm sure it's needed."

"Indeed." The sister stopped in front of a house with the number three on it. "Since Cottage Three is at the pool today, I'll show you theirs. Please, follow me."

They entered a small living room with a sofa bed and a bunch of bean bags on the shaggy carpet. A flat-screen television sat on a table across the room.

"My childhood home had shelves like those." Ellen pointed to the open shelves dividing the kitchen from the living area.

The kitchen was small, but tidy, with four upper cabinets, six lower, and linoleum floors and Formica countertops. Off the kitchen was a nook with a small table—not enough for twelve people—and a washer and dryer. Past the kitchen was another living area with three sofas, more bean bags, and another flat-screen television, though this one was mounted to the wall. The back door led to a small patio with not much of a yard between it and the street.

"That was once the front door," Sister Martha explained. "We converted the homes to face one another so they could share a larger common area."

"That was smart," Sue said.

The sister waved them back to the first living area to a hall that led to three bedrooms and two baths. Each room had three beds—one twin and a set of bunkbeds. The space was tight, but Ellen supposed the children were happier living in family-style homes rather than in institutions.

"Do the house parents live here full time?" Ellen wondered as they followed the nun back outside.

"No. They work three weeks on and one week off. These are often older couples whose own kids are grown, or they were couples who never had children of their own, or they're young and haven't yet started their own families. Well, we do have one couple with a baby, and the baby lives with them in the cottage while they're working."

"Where do they live when they're not working?" Sue wanted to know.

"We house them in apartments not too far from campus. They share with two other couples, but they're never there at the same time. For the week that they have the apartment, they are the only couple living there. So, it's not a glamorous living, but they get room, board, and a modest stipend, along with free medical."

As they neared the administrative building, two little girls—one black and the other white—ran up to Ellen and her friends with wildflowers they'd picked from the yard. They offered each of them a small bouquet.

Ellen gave each girl a smile. "How sweet. Thank you."

"Yes, thank you so much," Sue said.

Tanya sniffed hers. "They smell so good. Thank you."

"Can we pet your dog?" one of the girls asked.

"Sure, you can." Ellen bent over, so the girls could reach Moseby in his cloth pooch carrier. "He would like that very much."

"What's his name?" the other girl asked.

"Moseby," Ellen replied. "Or Mo for short."

"I like that," the first girl said as she gingerly stroked Mo.

"Okay, girls," Sister Martha said. "Go find your families."

The two girls giggled and scurried away.

"Aren't they sweet?" Tanya said without inflection. "They seem happy, too."

"We try our best," Sister Martha said.

"Well, you must be doing something right," Sue said with a grin.

Ellen wondered how much more they could be doing if Margaret had succeeded in getting the mafia money into the hands of the orphanage.

CHAPTER SIXTEEN

The Wait

Over the next few days, Ellen and her friends tried to be patient as they waited for news from Trina by distracting themselves with good food and fun entertainment at the beach and casinos. On Thursday afternoon, they visited the Bellissimo Spa at the Harrah's Gulf Coast Hotel and Casino and had massages, manicures, and pedicures. When Ellen's manicurist learned that Ellen and her friends were paranormal investigators, she told them a story about twins who always appeared at the foot of your bed in the old hospital just before you were about to die. Ellen asked the woman if she'd ever heard of Angelique Fayard, and the woman nodded.

"My grandfather told me that she's the ghost at the lighthouse," the manicurist said. "But she doesn't look out on the gulf. She looks toward the land, watching over Biloxi."

Each evening, with either a pitcher of margaritas or a bottle of wine, the three friends reviewed the footage they'd recorded on their full-spectrum cameras and listened to their EVP recordings. Although the cameras recorded the blood words and sentences written in the planner by the ghost of Mike Gillich and picked up the *yes* that

Tanya had heard whispered in her ear, they found nothing else of any consequence.

Thursday evening, out of curiosity, they visited the graves of Vincent and Margaret Sherry. They weren't interred at Old Biloxi Cemetery. They were down the road another six minutes, just before the Beauvoir, at Southern Memorial Park. Unlike Old Biloxi, which was on a hill shaded by ancient oaks through which winding paths meandered between massive headstones, Southern Memorial was flat and sunny with only a few short palm trees to break up the landscape. It was also more orderly with mostly flat headstones laid out on a grid. The ground was sandier here, too, with the gulf in plain sight. It was like being buried at the beach. Ellen supposed true lovers of the coast would relish the idea of relaxing on the beach for all eternity.

Ellen and her friends found the headstone with husband and wife buried together, and they prayed for the Sherrys and hoped they were at peace.

From there, they drove to the Back Water Bay of Biloxi, where the Sherrys were murdered. From their research, Ellen and her friends had discovered that the house, which had sat vacant since the Sherrys' deaths in 1987, had been destroyed by Hurricane Katrina and was later demolished. Now there was only an empty lot of grass at the place the Sherrys once called home.

Sue pulled up to the lot just as the sun was sinking on the horizon. The other homes on the street were nicely kept middle-class ranch-style homes built in the seventies and eighties—not too unlike Ellen's own house in San Antonio. Mature trees lined the street. Green lawns stretched from one end of the long block to the next, with utility poles lining the street and driveways laid on the flat terrain. Sue parked beneath two trees at the edge of the empty lot.

"Well, this is it," Sue said.

Tanya yawned. "Are we going to get out and walk around?"

Ellen opened her car door. "I'm sure Mo wouldn't mind a walk. Anyone want to join us?"

"My feet are killing me," Sue said. "Y'all go on without me."

Tanya climbed from the passenger's side of the Pilot. "We'll be right back."

Because she was at that age where she did what she wanted to unless someone told her she couldn't, Ellen led Moseby and Tanya across the empty lot, to see if she could sense any unrest from the spirit world.

"I hope no one says anything to us," Tanya muttered.

"We'll be fine," Ellen assured her.

Mo sniffed around and peed, happy to be out and about. The summer air was hot, but there was a breeze, and with the sun nearly gone from the horizon and dust blanketing them, it was rather nice.

Although the lot had appeared empty, Ellen noticed a woman with a pair of shears clipping away at a line of hedges at the back of the property. Moseby noticed her too and stood still, staring at her.

Tanya touched Ellen's hand and pointed, indicating that they should turn back and go the other way.

Ellen was about to follow Tanya when she changed her mind.

"Excuse me," she said to the woman.

The woman turned to her. "It can't have been for nothing. It just can't have been!"

"I'm sorry?" Ellen asked.

The woman turned back to the hedges and then she and her shears faded away.

Ellen couldn't speak for several seconds.

"Ellen?" Tanya called from a few yards away. "Aren't you coming?"

Moseby continued to stare in the direction of where the woman had appeared. He seemed to be as stunned as Ellen was.

"Ellen?"

Shaking, Ellen turned to Tanya and pointed at the empty hedge line. "She vanished into thin air. I think it was Margaret."

"What?" Tanya gaped. "What makes you think it was Margaret?"

"For one, she looked like the pictures we've seen on the internet. But also, she said, *It can't have been for nothing.*"

"It can't have been for nothing?" Tanya repeated. "You think she's talking about the stolen money?"

"The stolen money, their deaths, the impact it all had on their families and on Biloxi. Tanya, I think Margaret needs closure. We've got to find that money. We've got to do it for Margaret."

When they were in the Pilot and had told Sue about what the apparition had said, Sue shook her head. "But it you think about, it wasn't all for nothing. The murder investigation ended with the godfather of Biloxi behind bars. That had to have weakened the Dixie Mafia."

"I think she was talking about the money," Ellen argued. "I think she wanted it to go to the orphans of Biloxi."

"I wish there was a way we could make that happen," Tanya said. "But won't the authorities confiscate it?"

"I guess so," Ellen admitted.

"Why don't we say a prayer for Margaret before we go?" Sue suggested.

The ladies bowed their heads while Sue asked God and the heavenly angels to show Margaret the way, to help her find peace and comfort and rest. Then the three friends returned to their summer rental, where Ellen called Brenda, the homeowner, to let her know that the house had been spiritually cleansed and that they needed to stay there for at least another week to tie up some loose ends. Ellen offered to pay the going rate for the remainder of their stay, and Brenda accepted with gratitude.

Friday morning, Ellen and her friends were eating breakfast croissants out on their balcony when Ellen's phone rang.

"It's Trina!" Ellen said just before she accepted the call. Into the phone, she said, "Hello?"

"I told you ladies not to tell anyone about the nun."

Ellen glanced at her friends with a furrowed brow. "We haven't told a soul, except you. Why? Has something happened?"

"You haven't heard?"

"Heard what?" Ellen's stomach felt queasy as she put the phone on speaker and anxiously awaited the attorney's explanation.

"Someone dug up the nun. It's all over the news. It must have happened Wednesday night."

Ellen jumped to her feet. "What? How? I don't understand."

Her friends looked at her with wide eyes.

"Oh, my gawd," Sue whispered.

Tanya sat forward in her chair. "I can't believe this."

"Who would do that?" Ellen wondered.

"That's what I want to know," Trina replied. "You sure you told no one?"

"I'm sure," Ellen insisted. "Did they get the key?"

"If she was wearing it when she was buried, it's not on her now," the attorney replied. "Do you have any idea which bank the key belongs to?"

"No. None. Do you?" Ellen asked.

"Listen, it may be a while before I can arrange that meeting with Nix—if I can manage it all. You ladies might want to go home. There's nothing more you can do here in Biloxi. Besides, Nix is at the federal prison in Oklahoma. Didn't you say you were from Texas?"

"Yes, that's right," Ellen confirmed, still trying to process what Trina Gillich had revealed. "Do you have any idea who might have done this?"

"If you swear you didn't talk to anyone—"

"I swear."

"Damn. I'll have to call you back."

The call ended.

"You know what this means," Sue said without inflection as Ellen paced on the balcony.

Ellen stopped to face her friends. "Someone Trina's associated with is dirty. Maybe the judge? Or someone in her law office? Like an assistant?"

"What can we do to stop them from getting the money?" Tanya wondered. "Should we go to the police and tell them what we know? Call all the banks in town and warn them?"

Sue tapped a finger to her chin. "Ellen, why don't you call Trina back and ask what we should do? Tell her we want to do whatever we can to help."

"Are we sure we can trust her?" Tanya wondered. "Her father was the godfather of Biloxi. Maybe the apple didn't fall far from the tree."

"This is exactly why Margaret didn't turn the money over to the cops," Sue insisted. "She knew it would end up in the wrong hands."

"I don't know what to do," Ellen admitted. "I think I'll call Brian and get his advice."

"Good idea," Tanya said. "I'll call Priestess Isabel and ask her to throw the bones."

"I'll call Tom and make sure he isn't spending time with Rhonda."

Ellen ignored Sue's bad joke and took Moseby to her bedroom for some privacy while she made her call. She lay on the bed with Mo curled beside her and waited for Brian to answer.

"Well, hello there," he said.

A smile split her face in half. "Hello to you, too."

"I wasn't expecting to hear from you until tonight. What a pleasant surprise."

"Well, if I'm going to get this kind of greeting when I call in the morning, I'll have to do it more often."

"Please, do. Did you call to tell me that Tanya hit the jackpot?"

"No, I'm afraid not."

"I forgot to ask last night how your spa day went."

"Wonderful. You should see my toes."

"Ooh. Phone sex. Good idea."

Ellen threw her head back and laughed. "I'm actually calling because I need your advice."

"Sounds serious."

"I'm afraid it is."

Ellen filled him on in what had transpired.

"You girls need to come home. Sounds like a toxic environment. Let them sort it out for themselves."

"You really think so? It feels like unfinished business."

"You said Gillich moved on, right?"

Ellen sighed. "We believe so. But I think the ghost of Angelique Fayard is counting on us to find that money." She didn't mention Margaret's restless spirit, too.

"Sounds like it won't be long before someone else finds it."

"The wrong someone else."

"Let the cops sort that out, Ellen. Will you? I don't want to be a widower quite yet."

Ellen grinned. "But eventually."

"Heck yeah. We didn't sign a prenup." He chuckled.

As he was the one with the billions, his joke didn't make much sense—though her gold and oil money had certainly added to his assets since they married.

"Alright. I'll tell Sue and Tanya it's time to throw in the towel."

"I'll keep the light on for you."

"Love you."

"Love you, too. Kiss Moseby for me."

"Will do."

Ellen ended the call and kissed Moseby on his head.

Just then, Tanya opened the door with a distraught look on her face.

"Tanya? What's happened?"

"Priestess Isabel says we're in danger. We need to leave *now*."

CHAPTER SEVENTEEN

On the Run

"I'm all packed," Ellen said as she re-entered the main living area from her bedroom a half hour after her phone call with Brian had ended. "It just feels wrong, doesn't it?"

"I do feel unsettled," Sue admitted from where she sat in a wingback chair. "I hope we hear from Trina soon."

"It's disappointing, for sure." Tanya stretched out on the chaise lounge. "Where should we have dinner later? Let's pick something good, to cheer ourselves up."

Moseby jumped up beside Tanya.

She scratched behind his ears. "Hey, Moseby. Does that feel good?"

The earliest flight out of Gulfport-Biloxi International Airport wasn't until ten-thirty that night. Although there was an eight o'clock flight out of New Orleans, Sue would rather not drive the extra hour it would take to get there, especially at night, when her vision wasn't at its best.

"If I'd known this was going to be our last day here," Ellen began, "I'd have made a reservation at Mary Mahoney's."

"Maybe we can eat in the courtyard again," Sue speculated. "Well, probably not on a Friday night. Let me give them a call and see what they say."

"Did I just hear a car pull up?" Tanya climbed to her feet and went out onto the balcony.

Sue straightened her back. "I thought I heard a car door just now." She turned to Ellen. "Were you expecting Brenda and John to come by?"

Before Ellen could say no, Tanya re-entered. "Someone's parked behind us—two men. They're on their way to the side door. One of them is wearing a ski mask. What if they're from the mafia?"

"Oh, my gawd," Sue cried. "Priestess Isabel warned us about this. We need to get out of here."

Ellen scooped up Moseby. "Leave your things and let's go."

"But they're already down there. The stairwell has those big windows. They'll see us," Tanya pointed out. "What do we do?"

"I'm calling 9-1-1." Sue took out her phone and frantically tapped it. "We need to hide. Is that door locked?"

Ellen rushed to secure the door to the stairwell.

"What about the dumbwaiter?" Tanya suggested. "We could go down one at a time."

"You said they're parked behind us, though," Ellen pointed out.

"Yes, this is Sue Graham calling from 1022 Beach Boulevard," Sue said into the phone. "We have two intruders trying to break their way in." Then to Tanya, she insisted, "Go up instead of down. We can hide upstairs. That will buy us time until the police get here."

"You go first, Tanya," Ellen said just as the doorbell rang from downstairs. "I'll stall."

"Are you sure?" Sue asked.

Ellen wasn't sure, but she nodded anyway.

Her friends hurried to the kitchen.

"Who's there?" Ellen said into the speaker as Moseby, sensing how nervous she was, began to bark.

"Detective Jones and Miller with the Biloxi PD," a man's voice rang through. "We want to ask you a few questions."

Ellen wondered if it were at all possible that these men really were detectives. No, only a crook would wear a ski mask in this heat.

"Open the door, please," the man insisted. "We need to come up and speak with you."

"Of course, of course," Ellen cried. "I just need to put on some clothes. Give me one second, and I'll let you up."

Ellen rushed to the kitchen to see Sue entering the empty dumbwaiter.

"Hurry!" Ellen whispered as Sue struggled to pull her legs in.

"Help me," Sue insisted with a face as white as a sheet. "I'm not sure if I can fit. What if I can't fit?"

"You can fit." Ellen crossed through the kitchen and quickly pushed Sue's legs into the small elevator before closing her inside and pushing the button. She closed her eyes and said a prayer that the elevator could hold the extra weight.

A knock on the second-floor door made her jump out of her shoes. How had they made it past the first door?

"Lady, we don't have all day!" one of the men shouted. "Open up, now!"

"I'm coming! I'm coming!" she insisted, as she anxiously waited for the dumbwaiter to return.

Moseby whined in her arms. She kissed his head. "It's going to be okay, boy."

The men began pounding on the door. "Open this door, or we'll do it for you!"

"I just need to put my dog away. He's an attack dog, and I wouldn't want him to hurt you. Just another moment, please!"

She heard the men pound forcefully on the door, attempting to bust it open. She wondered if she should continue waiting for the dumbwaiter or run into one of the bedrooms to hide. What if they caught her before she and Moseby could climb inside?

A shot rang out. And then another. Ellen opened the dumbwaiter just as it returned. She climbed inside, scraping her arm and bumping her head, but she could barely feel it as she reached out and pushed the button before sliding the door closed. Holding her hand over Moseby's muzzle to stifle his whines, she prayed that she would make it to the third floor undetected.

She was still in transit when she heard the door to the stairwell burst open and the two men charge inside the second-floor unit. Would she and Mo make it before they were discovered?

The ride up seemed to take forever, but she hadn't made it all the way through the "Lord's Prayer" when the doors opened, and Tanya peered inside.

"You made it," Tanya whispered. "Be careful getting out. These floors creak."

Ellen whispered, "It won't take them long to figure out where we are."

"This way." Sue beckoned as she entered the hallway behind the fireplace.

Tanya had been right about the floors. They creaked with every step. Ellen took long, soft strides on her toes to soften the sound.

"There's a closet back here," Sue whispered of the first bedroom they came to, which was on the opposite side of the house from where Mike Gillich had been haunting the planner.

They could hear the men slamming doors below them and calling out for them. They tip-toed as quickly as they could across the room.

As Ellen and her friends squeezed together in the walk-in closet, Moseby kept whining and seemed on the verge of growling, too.

"Stop it, Mo!" Ellen snapped. "You're gonna get us caught!"

"How can you make him be quiet?" Tanya, her eyes wide with fear, asked. "They're going to hear him."

"You two better hide someplace else," Ellen, who was in the back of the closet, said. "I'll stay here with Mo."

"Are you sure?" Tanya asked.

It only took a nod from Ellen for Tanya to take off down the hall to the middle bedroom.

"Looks like we're in this together," Sue whispered.

"I appreciate it, Sue." Ellen gave her a worried smile.

"Oh, don't thank me. If I were in shape like Tanya, I'd run, too."

Under different circumstances, Ellen would have laughed, but as it was, she could hear the men climbing the stairs toward the third floor.

"Here they come," Sue whispered. "Brace yourself."

"Mo, please stop," Ellen said desperately as she held her dog close and covered his muzzle. "Sshh. It's okay, boy. You want a treat? You want some cheese?"

He stopped growling and looked at her for the first time. His little tail began to wag. Ellen prayed he would stay like that.

"The police should be here any minute," Sue whispered.

Ellen put a finger to her lips, for the men had entered the third floor.

"We know you're up here," one of them called. "You might as well come out. We just have a few questions for you."

When the men neared the bedroom where Ellen and Sue were hiding, Mo started barking ferociously.

"Come on out of there," one of the men said.

"You stay," Ellen whispered to Sue.

"Both of you," the man insisted.

Sue and Ellen stepped out of the closet. Ellen could barely feel her legs as she held her barking dog. Both men wore ski masks.

One was tall with broad shoulders. The short one was wiry and had a brown beard that peeked out beneath his mask.

"It's okay, Moseby-Mo," Ellen said in her sweetest voice, trying to keep him—all of them—from getting shot.

"Just tell us where the money is, and we'll be on our way," the short one demanded.

"We don't know," Ellen said with a shaky voice.

"What she meant to say," Sue began, "Is what money? But I guess it's too late for that."

"Aren't you a funny one," the short man said. "But if she'd said that, I would have shot her on the spot."

The short man glanced at the tall one, who seemed mute. Ellen realized the short man had been doing all the talking.

"Come on, ma'am," he complained to Ellen. "We know you know where it is. Otherwise, why would you hide from us?"

"At least he called you ma'am," Sue pointed out. "I think there's a special place in hell for crooks and murderers with good manners."

Ellen supposed everyone reacted differently under stress. Sue moved into attack mode. Ellen wanted to crawl into a hole.

"Listen," Ellen began, trying to be brave. "We have no idea what bank that key goes to. If we did, we'd tell you, I promise. We just want to go home. We don't want the money."

The two men seemed highly agitated. The tall one kicked a loose floorboard across the room.

"The safety deposit box was empty," the short man said.

Ellen and Sue exchanged looks of surprise.

"What?" Sue gawked. "That can't be."

"You think I'm lying?" he asked angrily as he moved closer to Sue and looked down his chest at her. "You think I'm making shit up?"

"No, sir," she said, "but I think I may have just shit my britches. I apologize in advance for any odor you may experience."

Both men backed away as they shook their heads with frustration. Ellen imagined that beneath their ski masks, they wore looks of disgust.

Then, they stood still at the sounds of footfalls on the stairwell.

"Someone's coming," the short guy said. To the women, he asked, "Did you call the cops?"

"I thought *you* were the cops," Sue said brazenly.

The short man pointed his gun right at Sue's face. Sue closed her eyes as her entire body rippled in one great shudder. Ellen thought her friend was going to collapse.

"Please don't!" Ellen cried. "What good will it do? It will only add to your problems!"

"Let's get out of here," the tall guy said.

So, he wasn't mute after all.

The short one started pacing. "There's only one way out and in."

"The dumbwaiter," Ellen said. "That's how we got past you. It's that way."

The men fled.

Ellen sighed with relief and put an arm around Sue. "You okay?"

"I don't know. You?"

"Yeah. I hope Tanya's alright."

"Why did you tell them about the dumbwaiter?" Sue wanted to know. "Now they might get away."

"They were going to take us as hostages," Ellen said. "That's what desperate crooks do in the movies, anyway."

"Biloxi PD!" an officer called from the hallway.

"They went down the dumbwaiter!" Sue cried.

The officer glanced inside the room, put a finger to his lips, and disappeared.

A moment later, Tanya emerged in the doorway. "Are you guys alright?"

"We think so," Ellen said. "You?"

"Fine, just in shock. You won't believe what happened while I was hiding in the closet next door."

Sue put her hands on her hips. "Well, you better tell us then."

"Someone whispered in my ear again," Tanya said, her face as white as chalk. "She said *in the ground*."

CHAPTER EIGHTEEN

Gulfport-Biloxi International Airport

It had taken forever to give their statements to the Biloxi police after the incident at their summer house rental, leaving Ellen and her friends no time to get dinner before heading to the airport. And the only restaurant they found once they got there was Sonic.

Ellen didn't mind Sonic. A grilled cheese and tater tots would have been fine on any other day. But she had been looking forward to one more evening of fresh seafood smothered in sauce on a bed of homemade pasta.

But worse than the lack of dinner options was the fact that one of the two men in ski masks had gotten away. Ellen found herself looking over her shoulder every few minutes. Her friends were doing the same.

They were eating their Sonic at the gate when Tanya said, "I wonder if Angelique wasn't talking about the key when she said *in the ground*. Maybe she was talking about the money."

Sue stopped her fry in mid-air and turned to Tanya. "Oh, my gawd! I think you're right."

"But how does that help us?" Ellen wanted to know. "If the money is in the ground, it could be buried anywhere."

"Except that Sister Anna Celeste's cat died two days before she did," Sue pointed out. "What if she buried it with her cat?"

Ellen shuddered and decided not to eat her last tater tot. The thought of a cat corpse buried with the money made her nauseous. Moseby was happy to eat the tater tot instead.

Tanya sat forward. "Bob must have been in on it, right? Bob Mahoney? Sister Anna Celeste was in her seventies, and I doubt she could have buried anything on her own."

Ellen's back stiffened. "Does that mean Bob Mahoney stole the money?"

The three friends sat there, pondering the possibilities.

After a few minutes, Sue took out her phone. "I think I'll call the restaurant and see if he's still there. Maybe I can feel him out."

Tanya grabbed Sue's phone from her. "Wait. Are you sure that's a good idea? What if he's in the Dixie Mafia?"

Ellen scratched her head. "If he stole the money, he'd be on their hit list."

"He would be, if anyone knew about it," Sue said. "Evidently, no one ever found out. I just want to see what he says before we go accusing anyone."

Tanya returned the phone to Sue. "Fine, but be careful. If he finds out we're on to him, he may want to kill us, too."

Ellen looked over her shoulder again, to make sure there was no one within listening distance. Thank goodness the airport was small and not heavily populated.

Sue found the number to the restaurant on her phone and made the call. "Hello, is Bob Mahoney still there, and if so, could I speak with him, please?"

"Put it on speaker," Tanya whispered. "There's no one around to overhear."

Sue put the phone on speaker in time for them to hear the employee who had answered say, "It'll take me a few minutes to find him. Do you want to hold that long?"

"Yes, I'll hold," Sue replied.

Ellen's stomach was twisting into knots. This phone call could go very wrong. Hopefully she and her friends could hop on their plane and get the heck out of Dodge before anyone came for them.

But how far a reach did the Dixie Mafia have? Could they come after Ellen and her friends and their families in San Antonio?

Ellen shuddered again as a bead of sweat formed on her forehead. "I hope we're not being stupid."

"Well, I hope that about you every day," Sue teased. "As for me, I'm being smart."

"This is Bob Mahoney," Bob's familiar voice rang out over the phone.

"Hi Bob, this is Sue. I'm the one who asked you to take a photo with me last week, to make my husband jealous?"

"You'd be surprised how many women ask me to pose in pictures with them. Heck, *I'm* more surprised than anyone."

"My friends and I asked you about Sister Anna Celeste?"

"Oh, yes, our Nun of the Above. I remember you now. What can I do you for?"

"My friends were wondering if you could tell us more about Sister Anna Celeste's cat—the one you helped her with before she died. I'm writing a blog post about my mother's friends in Biloxi, and anything you could tell me would be ever so helpful."

"I never met her cat. She called her Dixie. She was a feral cat and didn't live in the convent. That's the way Sister Anna Celeste was. She took care of everyone and everything."

"Can you recall what the cat looked like?" Sue asked.

"I never saw it."

Sue glanced at her friends with a look of confusion. "You never saw the cat?"

"When she asked me to help her bury Dixie, Sister Anna Celeste didn't want to trouble me anymore than she had to, so she'd already bundled the body in a bunch of old towels or a bag—I can't recall. I'm sorry I can't tell you more about it. And she was terrible at taking pictures. They didn't have cell phones back then, you know."

"Right," Sue replied. "How did we survive?"

"Aint' that the truth. We got lost a lot more often, that's for sure. Anything else I can do you for?"

Ellen leaned forward, "One more question, Bob. Hi, this is Ellen. Do you recall where Dixie is buried?"

"Well, it's against the homeowners' association rules, so she never liked people to know it, but she had a pet graveyard right there behind the convent. I buried Dixie beneath her favorite tree."

"Which tree was that?" Sue asked, catching on to Ellen's line of thinking.

"There was only one tree back there. Why is this important to your blog post?"

"Oh, you're right. It's not important," Sue said with a laugh. "My mom used to call me Curious George, because I never seem to know when to stop asking questions."

"My mom called me Chatty Cathy. You and me get along just fine."

"Thank you for your time, Bob. It was great meeting you."

"Y'all have a good night, ladies."

Sue ended the call.

Ellen could barely contain her excitement. "Do you think it's possible that the money was buried in the back yard of the convent? I don't think there ever was a cat, do you?"

"Keep your voice down," Sue said as she glanced around.

"I think it's possible," Tanya said. "But the more interesting question is, if so, is it still there?"

Sue balled up her trash from Sonic. "What do you guys think we should do?"

Ellen took Sue's trash and held out her hand for Tanya's.

Tanya handed hers over. "Thanks."

"Angelique wants us to find the money." Ellen stood up and tossed the garbage. When she returned to her seat, Tanya's brow was wrinkled.

"What's wrong, Tanya?" Ellen asked.

"I'm so sick of digging up graves."

Ellen laughed. "Me, too."

"Well." Sue straightened her back. "I think the bigger question is, if the money is still there, and if we dig it up—"

Tanya shot her a look. "We?"

"Yes, we." Sue insisted. "I can help, though with the cut on my hand, I'm not sure how much help I'll be."

Ellen lifted her hand. "I have the same cut."

"Great," Tanya muttered.

"Anyway," Sue continued. "The bigger question is, if we *were* to find the money, what would we do with it? Would we give it to the police?"

"Can we trust them?" Tanya wondered.

Sue tapped her chin. "I would think the cops of today are more trustworthy than the ones Margaret was dealing with, but I just don't know, especially with what happened to Sister Anna Celeste's grave. What if we go to all this trouble only to inadvertently return the money to the Dixie Mafia?"

"We need to finish Margaret's work," Ellen said. "We need to give the money to the Biloxi orphanage."

"Are we canceling our flights, then?" Tanya asked. "Should we go for it?"

"I think we'll regret it if we don't," Sue argued. "Don't you, Ellen?"

"Absolutely. We've gone this far. We can't leave this undone. It won't feel right."

Ellen's heart pumped with excitement as she followed her friends to the attendant's desk. "Here we go again, Moseby-Mo. We're about to get in way over our heads."

CHAPTER NINETEEN

Dog Trouble

"How many shovels and sets of gloves have we bought at Walmart over the years?" Sue wondered as she pushed the shopping cart down the aisle of the garden department.

"I've lost count," Ellen admitted. "But let's just get one and take turns. It's not like we're digging up a body this time."

A woman with a toddler gave Ellen a funny look.

"I'm more worried about getting caught by Sister Thusala," Tanya said.

Sue turned down the aisle with the shovels. "That's why we're going tonight while everyone's asleep."

Afraid to return to their summer house rental, lest the man in the ski mask who got away be there waiting for them, the three friends checked into a hotel in nearby Ocean Springs. They decided to wait there until midnight, when the nuns were sure to be in bed for the night.

A few minutes past the witching hour, Sue pulled the Honda Pilot into the parking lot across the street from the convent on Fayard Street. Ellen had left Moseby at their hotel with another chicken-flavored treat, worried that if he came along, he would bark and give them away.

Her hopes of avoiding a barking dog were dashed when two Pit bulls, growling and barking like the three heads of Cerberus in the mythological Underworld, appeared in the fenced yard of the house next door.

"Oh, great," Tanya whispered. "This isn't going to work."

"I wonder where they were when we visited the other day?" Sue said as she stood by the Pilot holding the shovel.

"Probably inside," Tanya pointed out.

"I've got Moseby's treats in the back. Maybe an offering will quiet them down."

"You might be offering more than the treats," Sue said. "You'll likely lose a hand along with them."

Ellen opened the hatchback and grabbed two handfuls of chicken-flavored treats. "I've got to try, haven't I? Or we've gone this far for nothing."

"Just be careful," Tanya said, as if Ellen planned to do anything else.

With fistfuls of treats, Ellen crossed the street and approached the fence, forcing a smile on her face. "Hello there, sweet things. You want a treat? You want a treat?"

They were familiar with the word, because as soon as she'd said it, they sat on their haunches and looked up at her quietly like two obedient little soldiers.

"Here's one for you, and here's one for you."

Unlike Mo, who could take all day to unravel, chew, and consume one treat, these dogs had theirs eaten in no time.

"What are y'all waiting for?" Ellen whisper-yelled to her friends who were hovering near the Pilot across the street. "Better get started!"

The dogs jumped up and began barking as soon as Tanya and Sue approached.

"You want a treat?" Ellen asked again.

Just like soldiers, the two dogs sat at attention, looking at her expectantly.

Ellen realized she'd have to take her time with the delivery of each treat, or she'd soon run out.

"Good girls," she said, having noticed they were females. "You want your treat, don't you?"

Tanya ran up to Ellen. "The gate on this side is padlocked shut. I wonder why. I'm going around."

"I want your job." Sue held the shovel up to Ellen. "Want to trade?"

Ellen rolled her eyes and had been about to complain that the hard part of this job was over—the risking your hand part—but instead realized that Sue, no matter how much she'd insisted otherwise, would not be able to dig.

"Fine." Ellen handed over the treats and took the shovel. "But make these last as long as you can. Keep saying treat, right girls? You want your treat?"

The dogs were eyeing the treats with much excitement and anticipation in their eyes while they sat at attention.

"Just try to hurry it up," Sue teased. "Dig fast."

"There are more of these in the car, if you run out," Ellen added before quickly and quietly crossing the yard and catching up with Tanya.

"This gate is padlocked, too," Tanya said. "I don't get it. I guess we'll have to climb over."

"Wonderful," Ellen said.

Tanya handed Ellen her flashlight and the pair of gloves before using her long legs to jump over in two moves.

Ellen handed the light, gloves, and shovel over to Tanya. "I don't know if I can do this."

"Sure, you can. You aren't making me dig by myself."

Ellen could not squeeze her wide shoe into the fence to gain purchase, nor could she lift her foot four feet to the top. So, she turned her backside to the fence, and attempted to pull herself up to a sitting position. But that, too, failed.

"I see a five-gallon bucket back here," Tanya said. "Hold on."

It was a sturdy, plastic bucket from Home Depot. Ellen stepped on it, put a foot on the top of the fence, and jumped over. She lost her balance and fell to her knees.

"Are you okay?" Tanya whispered.

"That hurt." Ellen used the fence to pull herself up. "That money better be there after all of this."

Together, they rushed across the yard to the one tree, which was on the side of the house with the Pit bulls. Hopefully they would be more interested in the treats than in what she and Tanya were up to.

"Where should I start?" Tanya wondered.

Ellen turned her headlamp on. Scattered beneath the tree were a half-dozen painted steppingstones. The one by her feet was painted *Fin*. Three feet away was another painted *Charlie*. Opposite it was one painted *Dixie*.

"There." Ellen pointed to the rock that said *Dixie*. "Start digging there."

Ellen held the flashlight and her headlamp pointed to the ground while Tanya stuck on the gloves and began digging. After she'd made a hole about a foot deep and two feet wide, she sighed and wiped her brow.

"Time to switch?" Ellen offered.

"Yes. This is exhausting. And it's so hot."

It did feel hotter here than it had on the strip near the gulf. Ellen took the gloves, handed over the flashlight, and took the shovel to try her hand at uncovering the lost money.

She hadn't been digging long when the Pit bulls came bounding along the fence to the back and started barking and growling at them again.

"Sue must have run out of treats."

A light turned on inside the convent followed by another on the outside over the backdoor.

"Oh, shit," Tanya muttered. "Run!"

Tanya took off along the fence, the dogs madly chasing her. Ellen dropped the shovel and attempted to follow when someone stepped out from the backdoor and cried, "Ellen?"

Ellen stopped in her tracks. It was Sister Bridget.

"You better come inside and tell me what you're doing here," the sister insisted.

At least she hadn't threatened to call the cops.

Ellen crossed the yard to the back door. "I'm so sorry, Sister. It's a long story."

"Come on inside and tell it, then."

As Ellen entered, she noticed the nun had a black eye. "Oh, my gosh! What happened to you?"

"I suppose we both have stories to tell."

Another light turned on in the main living area as Sister Thusala, still wearing her breathing tube along with a nightgown, emerged. "Sister Bridget? What's going on?"

Two more sisters appeared in their pajamas. One of them was Sister Martha from the orphanage, who was all neck and legs, only today she had a busted lip. The nun beside her was half her height and just as thin with red curly hair and freckles.

"Hello, sisters," Ellen smiled with embarrassment as her cheeks burned. "Can we let my friends inside? They can help me to explain."

Sister Bridget went to the front door, where Tanya and Sue were already waiting.

"I guess you're wondering why we're here." Sue stepped inside. "I wish I could say it was to sell you some Avon. Oh, Sister Martha! What happened? And Sister Bridget? Did you two get in a fight?"

"We're fine," Sister Martha insisted. "But please sit down and tell us why you've awakened us at this ungodly hour."

The sisters offered Ellen and her friends a seat on the couch and armchair. Sister Thusala took the wooden chair by the kitchen, and the three other nuns remained standing.

"This is Sister Rachel, by the way," Sister Martha introduced. To Sister Rachel, she added, "This is Sue, Ellen, and Tanya."

"Nice to meet you," the young nun said.

"Likewise," Sue said. "Though I wish it was under better circumstances."

"That's an understatement," Sister Thusala grumbled.

"You might want to sit down for this," Ellen said to the standing nuns.

"We're alright," Sister Bridget insisted. "Why don't you tell us what's going on?"

"It began in 1987," Sue explained. "Margaret Sherry stole a large sum of mafia money from her husband's law firm and secretly gave it to Sister Anna Celeste for the orphanage."

"What?" Sister Martha cried as all four nuns looked at one another as though aliens had invaded. "That can't be!"

Ellen pulled the note from her crossbody purse. "Margaret wrote this to Sister Anna Celeste just before she was killed. We found it in the sister's prayer book."

"You took it from her prayer book?" Sister Thusala admonished.

"I'm sorry, Sister," Sue said, "but we needed to show it to an attorney as proof. You can have it back now if you want it."

"It's a good thing you took it," Sister Bridget remarked. "That's exactly what those men came looking for yesterday."

"What men?" Ellen asked as adrenaline surged through her. She knew the answer before they said it.

"They wore ski masks," Sister Thusala explained.

Sister Bridget touched her black eye. "That's why I didn't call the police tonight when I heard someone on the property."

"They said they'd kill us if we involved the cops," Sister Martha added.

"They came after us, too," Tanya reported.

Sue scooted to the edge of the couch. "They were after the money. They thought you knew where it was, and they thought we knew where it was, but we didn't until tonight."

Sister Thusala narrowed her eyes. "And that's why you're here? You want the money?"

"Not for ourselves," Tanya said defensively. "We want to give it to the orphanage. Right, guys?"

"That's right," Ellen promised. "We hoped to fulfill Margaret's and Sister Anna Celeste's wishes, since they both died trying to do it themselves."

"What do you mean *both died trying to do it themselves*?" Sister Bridget repeated.

"Oh, gosh," Ellen said, glancing at her friends. "That's right. You don't know."

"Don't know what?" Sister Thusala demanded.

Ellen and her friends explained what they'd learned from the ghost of Mike Gillich.

Sister Bridget sat on the floor, trying to process the news. The other two nuns who'd been standing went to get chairs from the kitchen. They brought out a third for Sister Bridget.

"Poor Sister Anna Celeste." Sister Thusala covered her face and wept.

Sue frowned. "I'm so sorry to have been the bearer of bad news. So sorry you had to find out this way."

"If those men find out we had the money all along," Sister Martha said suddenly, "we're dead meat."

"We have a plan," Ellen announced. "That is, if the money's even there."

"Should we go find out?" Sister Rachel, the redhead who was quiet and small and young, suggested.

"Be on the lookout for those scoundrels," Sister Thusala warned. "If the girls start barking again, come on inside."

Sister Martha turned to Ellen and her friends, "After the men came and hurt us, we asked our neighbors if they'd keep their dogs out at night, in case the bad guys came back. That's why we were suspicious tonight when the girls started barking. We thought you were those evil men."

"Speaking of the dogs," Ellen began. "Isn't that them barking now?"

Sister Martha looked out of the front window while Sister Rachel looked out the back.

"There's someone back there!" Sister Rachel whispered. "It looks like he's digging up Dixie's grave!"

CHAPTER TWENTY

The Man in the Mask

Tanya jumped to her feet. "What should we do? We can't call the police."

"Maybe we *should* call the police," Sister Thusala argued. "Forget those threats."

"But Sister Thusala." Sister Martha crossed the room to the back window. "If we involve the police, they'll take the money."

Sister Rachel turned to Sister Martha, "What will they do with it?"

"If it's a federal crime, it goes to the federal government," Sister Bridget explained.

"Mail fraud is a federal crime," Sue pointed out. "That's where the money originally came from—the Lonely Hearts Scam."

"We want that money to go to the orphans of Biloxi," Sister Martha reiterated. "That means we can't involve the police." Then she made the sign of the cross. "Please, tell me that's the right thing to do, Sister Thusala, assuming the money's still there."

"The money's there," Sister Thusala said.

"What?" the others asked at once. "What do you mean?"

"How do you know?" Sister Bridget asked.

"Well, I didn't know it until tonight, but Sister Anna Celeste has been coming to my dreams regularly, asking me to dig up Dixie's grave, saying there was money buried there, and that there never was a cat named Dixie. I thought it was a crazy dream!"

Everyone in the room gasped.

Two of the nuns made the sign of the cross.

"She wants us to find the money!" Martha cried.

Ellen looked out the back window to see the man still digging. By the light of the back porchlight, she could tell that he was the taller and less talkative of the two masked men that had invaded their summer house rental.

"When Margaret Sherry decided to give the money to Sister Anna Celeste," Ellen began, "she was trying to take the moral high ground under the circumstances. I think that's what we've got to do, too. It might not be the legal thing to do, but, given that we don't know who to trust, it's the moral thing to do. We've got to go out there and overtake that man. There's one of him and seven of us."

Sue jerked her thumb toward the sisters. "What do you think they are? Nun-jas? We can't overpower him."

"Sure, we can," Ellen insisted. "If we plan it right."

Tanya peered through the back window. "Let him do the majority of the digging first."

"But he's got a gun," Sister Rachel, ignoring Tanya's comment, pointed out.

Sue reached her hand into her purse. "And so do I."

As she pulled out her gun, the nuns gawked.

"Whoa! Wait a minute!" Sister Bridget waved her arms. "Do you know how to use that thing?"

"Yes, I do."

Ellen and Tanya exchanged worried looks.

Sister Thusala used her oxygen cart to pull herself up to her feet. "This is a house of God. We have a consecrated host in here. You can't have that gun in this house of worship."

"Fine," Sue said. "I'll take it out there and use it."

"Sue, wait," Tanya warned. "Let's think of a plan first."

"I've got a plan," Sue argued. "I'm going to shoot him in the leg."

"Someone will hear the shot and call the cops," Sister Martha protested.

"Then I'll just *threaten* to shoot," Sue said. "He's worried about the cops being called, too, so he won't shoot either, right?"

"They fired at the door at our summer rental," Ellen reminded her.

"We have to do something!" Sue cried. "He's going to steal the money!"

Without waiting for another objection, Sue opened the back door and pointed her gun at the masked man.

Ellen's stomach was in knots, and her heart was exploding in her ears. She raced after Sue, hoping to pull her back inside, but she was too late.

"Stop right there, or I'll shoot," Sue shouted. "I'm an excellent shot, by the way. My shooting teacher said so and gave me a marksman award."

The man dropped the shovel and put his hands in the air. "Don't do anything stupid."

Before Ellen had even blinked, the man drew his gun on Sue. A shot fired. Ellen screamed, as did the other ladies in the convent. Ellen rushed through the door, expecting to see her friend on the ground, but it was the man in the mask who was injured and writhing in the grass. His gun had fallen out of his hand, and Sue was racing toward him with her gun pointed at him.

Ellen followed with Sisters Martha and Bridget on her heels. The man held a bloody shoulder and struggled to get up.

"Don't move!" Sue shouted. "If you don't want me to call the cops on you, you better hold it right there."

"You aren't gonna call the cops?" the man asked.

Sue stopped about three feet away from him. "No. I'm going to let you go. This is a house of mercy, so I'm going to show you some. But before I let you leave, I'll need you to remove your mask."

The man jumped to his feet, like he was going to make a run for it.

"You want me to shoot you in the foot?" Sue threatened.

The man stopped in his tracks. "Fine!" He used his good arm to pull the ski mask off.

"John?" Ellen cried.

"Oh, my gosh!" Tanya shouted from the doorway.

It was Brenda's husband, the landlord of their summer rental.

"Why on earth?" Sue cried.

"We lost a ton of money on that damn house," he spat. "All because of that stupid book. After all we went through? We *earned* that money in the ground. It should be ours."

"How did you know where to find it?" Ellen wanted to know.

"I overheard you ladies talking one night on the balcony. I'd come by to see if I could have the planner once you'd exorcised it."

"Because you thought it would lead you to the money," Sue accused.

"I can't believe you hit me!" Sister Martha shouted. "A servant of our lord!"

"That wasn't me. That was my brother-in-law."

"He's the one who was arrested?" Ellen asked, remembering the short man who had pointed his gun directly at Sue.

John nodded. "I was gonna split it with him. We're both in debt out the wazoo."

"There are better ways to get out of debt, John," Sister Thusala chastised from the back door.

"Why don't you sell the house?" Sue asked, though Ellen didn't think this was the time to try to solve the man's financial problems.

"We can't get what we paid for it."

"Did you and your brother-in-law dig up Sister Anna Celeste's grave?" Sister Thusala asked.

"We didn't mean any disrespect, Sister," John said. "I was desperate. Am desperate."

"We'll pray for you," Sister Thusala said. "But you should know that there are no shortcuts in life. Life is hard. Deal with it."

"Leave your gun and go," Sue ordered. "Before I change my mind."

The ladies watched as John hobbled across the yard and jumped the gate. The ladies hurried through the house to the front windows to see him continue down the road. Ellen ran out of the front door and watched him climb into a truck a few houses down and drive away.

As she ran back to the house, she told the others, "We better hurry, in case he changes his mind or brings back reinforcements."

"Or in case someone called the cops," Sister Martha added.

Sister Thusala waited in the doorway to the back yard as the others rushed to the dig site. Sue found John's gun and emptied it. Tanya grabbed the shovel. Ellen knelt over the hole and started digging with her hands.

She was surprised by how warm the soil was and was even more surprised when her fingers rubbed against fabric. "I feel something."

Tanya dropped the shovel and began digging with her hands, too. Soon the three nuns were helping while Sue watched over them, a gun in each hand.

Sister Martha caught a fabric handle. She tugged and tugged while the others loosened the soil around it. With her headlamp to see by, Ellen saw something taking shape in the dirt. It was a blue duffle bag about three feet long and wide.

The movements of the hands became more frantic. At last, the bag was out!

"Let's take it inside!" Sister Martha insisted as she and Sister Rachel lugged the heavy, dirt-caked bag to the house."

Sister Bridget ran ahead of them and laid a towel on the kitchen floor. "Over here."

Ellen and her friends watched with excitement as Sister Martha unzipped the bag and pulled the two sides apart. Then she removed a navy terry cloth towel. The suspense was killing Ellen.

Sister Martha chuckled. "Sister Anna divided the money into Ziplock bags."

"Thank heavens for Ziplock technology!" Sister Rachel cried as she pulled two bags out.

"How much is in there?" Sister Thusala wanted to know.

The ladies carried the plastic bags to the kitchen table and pulled the stacks of money free of them. As they continued to stack it on the table, Sue counted one of the stacks.

"Each stack has a hundred one-hundred-dollar bills," Sue said after a while.

"Each of these is a thousand dollars?" Sister Rachel asked with wide eyes. "But there are hundreds of them!"

The sisters quickly arranged the stacks in groups of ten.

"That's 120 total stacks of ten thousand each," Tanya said once they'd organized all the money.

"Oh, my Lord!" Sister Thusala cried. "That's one point two million!"

The three younger nuns began jumping up and down and hugging each other.

"Think of what this will do for your orphanage," Ellen said, her heart full.

"We need to stop celebrating and come up with a plan," Sue demanded, bringing everyone back to reality. "We've got to get this money out of here, in case the cops or John or anyone else comes looking for it."

"What do you suggest?' Sister Martha asked with a skeptical tone.

Ellen crossed her arms over her chest. "Our plan was to divide it between the three of us, check it on the plane in our luggage on the first flight out tomorrow, and deposit it into our individual accounts in San Antonio. Then we would purchase cashier's checks and mail them certified mail to the orphanage."

Sensing discord among the sisters, Sue asked, "You don't like that plan?"

The nuns frowned at one another.

"It's a reasonable plan," Sister Martha finally said. "But, well, we've dealt with a lot of sinners in our lives, and we barely know you. How can we trust you with all this money, money that was meant for our orphanage? Why shouldn't we deposit it in *our* account and then give a check to the orphanage?"

"You could," Sue began, "but you don't think that might look suspicious? You don't think the police will put it together? Sister Anna Celeste's body was found dug up, the key was missing from her body, and suddenly the convent has 1.2 million dollars?"

"How is your plan any less suspicious?" Sister Thusala asked.

"First of all," Sue began, "we are already millionaires. You might not be able to tell it by looking at us, but we've discovered gold and struck oil. If we each deposit whatever a third of 1.2 million dollars is—"

"Four hundred thousand," Tanya interjected.

"It won't draw any attention from our bankers," Sue explained. "We already deposit large sums in our accounts on a regular basis."

"And we also donate large sums on a regular basis, too," Ellen added.

"Your bank might bat an eye, sisters," Sue went on. "If you dump all this into your account, you're going to raise some red flags."

"I hadn't thought of that," Sister Martha admitted.

"And second of all," Sue continued, "we were planning to send the money to the orphanage in increments, each of us sending our share a month apart, starting six months from now, after all the hoopla over Sister Anna Celeste's grave has died down."

"That does sound smart, now that you've explained it," Sister Thusala confessed. "But you can imagine how nervous it makes us, can't you? You're asking us to put all our trust in you, and we're aware of how easily the human heart can be corrupted. We're completely vulnerable here."

"Are those sirens I hear?" Tanya asked suddenly.

Everyone stopped talking to listen.

Sure enough, sirens could be heard in the distance, and they were drawing nearer.

CHAPTER TWENTY-ONE

Devious Minds

"You better take the money and go," Sister Thusala said. "Hurry, before the police arrive."

"We need something less conspicuous to carry it in," Sue pointed out. "Got any luggage we can use? We promise to return it."

The three younger nuns dashed to their rooms, and each returned with a rolling suitcase. They opened the cases on the kitchen floor, and the ladies began tossing the stacks of money into them as quickly as they could.

"If anyone asks," Sister Martha said without looking up as she chunked more money into a case, "you were here praying a novena with us for the restful repose of Sister Anna Celeste."

"Got it," Sue agreed.

Ellen zipped up one of the cases. "Sue, give me the key. I'll bring the Pilot around. You and Tanya meet me at the end of the driveway."

Sue handed over the key, and Ellen made a run through the front door for the Pilot. The sirens sounded like they were only a block away. Ellen cranked the engine and pulled across the street to the drive, then, leaving the car running, she darted inside to lug one of the cases out as Tanya and Sue dragged the others. The younger three sisters helped them lift the cases into the hatchback and then rushed back inside. Ellen and her friends had barely made it into the Pilot when a police car pulled up, sirens blaring, to the curb in front of the house with the Pit bulls.

The dogs were going nuts.

"Kill the engine and wait," Ellen instructed from the backseat. "We'll leave once they're inside the other house."

"What if they don't go in?" Tanya wondered.

"Just hold on a minute," Ellen insisted. "We'll look too suspicious if we leave right now."

"Oh, no," Sue groaned. "One of the officers is coming this way."

"Roll down your window and act dumb," Ellen said.

"It won't be an act," Sue complained as she rolled down the window. "I'm so scared, I can barely think."

"Good evening," an officer, female and black, asked as she approached the side of the Pilot with her flashlight shining.

"Good evening, Officer," Sue replied. "Everything okay?"

"That's what I was about to ask you. We received a report of a gunshot and suspicious activity in this area from the house next door. Do you know anything about that? Who's in the car with you?"

Ellen rolled down the backseat window. "Hello. I'm Ellen. Those are my friends Sue and Tanya. We were just here with the sisters praying a novena for the repose of our dear friend Sister Anna Celeste, whose body—"

"Yes, I heard about that. I'm so sorry that happened to your friend," the officer said. "How did you know the sister?"

"She was a friend of my mother's," Sue replied without missing a beat. "That's what brought me to Biloxi. My mother recently passed and, from reading her diary, I discovered he made some good friends here. Well, I wanted to meet them, if I could."

"So, you ladies heard no gunshot?"

"We heard something that sounded like a gunshot," Sue confessed, "but I thought it was a car backfiring."

"I thought it was a firecracker," Tanya said from the passenger's seat. "I thought maybe people in Biloxi start celebrating July 4th early."

"No ma'am," the officer said with a laugh. "We celebrate it the same as everyone else."

"Do you think it really was a gunshot?" Ellen asked the officer, who had begun to shine her light into the back of the vehicle.

"That's what we're hoping to find out," the officer replied. "Are you ladies going somewhere? Looks like you got your bags packed."

"We're not from here," Sue explained. "We're just visiting from San Antonio."

"San Antonio, huh? Where are you staying?"

"At a hotel in Ocean Springs," Ellen replied.

"We were staying at a summer rental on Beach Boulevard," Sue clarified, "but there was a break in—you may have heard of it—and so we didn't feel safe there anymore."

"I did hear about that," the officer said with narrowed eyes. "Trouble seems to follow you ladies, huh?"

Ellen laughed nervously. "I wouldn't say that. That was the first time I've ever experienced anything like that. Did you ever find out why they did it?"

"Money," the officer said. "It's almost always about money."

Tanya gave Ellen a worried glance. Ellen hoped the officer hadn't noticed it.

"Well, we have an early flight, officer," Sue said. "Unless you have any more questions, we'd like to get back to our hotel."

"Get back to it?" the officer asked. "You're already checked in?"

"Yes, ma'am," Ellen confirmed.

"Then why is your luggage still in the back?"

"Oh," Ellen said, trying to think, "we were in a hurry."

"Our flight leaves early in the morning," Sue added. "So, we just took in our smaller bags—you know, our cosmetic cases and a change of clothes for the morning."

"Which is it?" the officer asked.

"Excuse me?" Sue tilted her head to the side.

"Is your luggage back there because you were you in a hurry? Or was it because of the early morning flight?"

"Both," Ellen said quickly. "We didn't want to lug all of our suitcases in for just one night, but we were also in a hurry to get here to the sisters, so we could pray the novena."

"That's right," Sue confirmed. "We didn't want them to start without us."

"What time did you get here?" the officer asked.

"It was really late," Sue said. "Must have been close to midnight."

Ellen nodded, remembering the advice Sue's mother had once given them: If you had to lie to save your hide, keep it as close to the truth as possible.

"What time did you check in at the hotel in Ocean Springs—which hotel is it?"

"The Wingate by Wyndham," Ellen replied. "We checked in around nine o'clock, I believe, or shortly after."

"Then why did it take you so long to get here?"

"We fell asleep," Sue said quickly. "We only meant to lay our heads down for a minute, and luckily Tanya here woke up and got us up."

"That's when we decided not to bother bringing in the rest of the luggage," Ellen added, "because we were already running late."

"You were going to bring it in and then decided not to?"

"That's right," Sue said. "It wasn't worth it, since we are flying out in the morning, and we were in a hurry."

"What flight are you flying out on?"

Ellen noticed the other officer approaching the convent door.

"Oh, gosh," Sue fumbled. "I don't remember. Do you, Tanya?"

"I can look it up," Tanya offered as she pulled out her phone and began tapping at the screen.

"Do you remember the airline?" the officer asked.

"Delta, wasn't it?" Ellen asked Sue.

"Or was that the airline we rode in on?" Sue wondered.

"You didn't get a round trip ticket?"

"We flew into New Orleans, to see a friend," Ellen explained. "We had a return flight from here but then we decided to stay longer, so we forfeited the round trip and haven't purchased the return trip yet. We're hoping to fly out on standby."

"It is Delta," Tanya confirmed. "It leaves at six-thirty in the morning."

"Goodness, then you ladies better get a move on. That's only four hours from now."

"Thank you, officer." Sue put the Pilot in reverse and began to back out.

"I have your names and numbers from your statements after the break in," the officer said. "If I have any more questions, I'll be in touch."

"Of course," Sue said. "Good night."

"Good night."

The three friends were as silent as stones as Sue backed out and drove away from the convent. They were already on the bay bridge headed for Ocean Springs when Ellen could speak again.

"Oh, my gosh, was that terrifying or what?" she asked.

"I don't think we're out of the woods yet," Sue said from behind the wheel. "That officer was mighty suspicious."

"With good reason," Ellen conceded.

Tanya glanced back at Ellen. "We better be at that airport when we said we would be. She might be waiting there for us."

"I just hope to God she won't be waiting there with handcuffs," Sue said.

Ellen couldn't agree more. "I do *not* like this feeling of being on the wrong side of the law."

"Remember what you said about the difference between doing the legal thing and the moral thing?" Tanya said. "Have you changed your mind? It's a little late for that."

Sue turned into the parking lot of their hotel. "Oh, look. There's a Waffle House across the street. I'm starving. Anyone want to go eat?"

"Moseby's been alone too long as it is," Ellen objected.

"I'm too nervous to eat," Tanya said.

"I wish I had that problem," Sue said with a sigh. "When I'm nervous, all I want to do is eat. But alright, fine. I'll starve."

"I guess we're leaving the money in the car?" Ellen asked. "All one point two million dollars?"

"Hells, bells," Sue said. "What else can we do?"

"Park over there, under that streetlamp," Tanya suggested. "Maybe it will deter criminals."

"Are we worried about criminals or cops?" Ellen asked, confused.

"Oh, my gawd," Sue said suddenly. "What if John's been following us? What if he tries to steal the money away from us while we're sleeping in the hotel?"

"I would think he'd be at the emergency room," Tanya said.

"I don't think so," Sue argued. "Because then he'd have to explain why he has a bullet in his shoulder. No, he went home and plucked that bullet out himself. Maybe he got Brenda to clean and stitch the wound."

Ellen glanced around the parking lot. "Oh, heavens. What should we do?"

Sue pulled beneath the streetlamp. "Maybe we should get our things and go to the airport now. The sooner we can check our bags, the better."

Tanya covered her mouth. "What if they lose our luggage? That happens sometimes, doesn't it? It happened to Dave once."

Ellen hugged her belly. "I feel sick."

"This is crazy," Sue cried. "We're not doing anything bad . . . we're trying to help orphans. Why should this be so stressful? If my money weren't tied up in real estate and other investments, I'd just give the orphanage the one point two million and leave this money for the cops to find."

"Same," Ellen said.

"Maybe we should go to the police," Tanya wondered out loud.

Ellen snapped her head up and glared at Tanya. "After all we just went through to *avoid* involving the police? Are you crazy?"

"They'll arrest us, for sure," Sue argued.

"Maybe we should call Trina and tell her everything," Tanya suggested.

"That's the worst idea I've heard yet," Sue complained. "If she's dirty, she'll turn us over to the Dixie Mafia, and if she's clean, she'll turn us into the police."

"Oh, lord." Ellen hugged her belly again. Then she said, "Let's do this. Let's take the money up to the room with us, divide it up between all our other bags, mixing it in with clothes and whatnot. Then, we'll load everything back in the car and head for the airport. This way, if a bag gets lost, it won't be a huge loss."

"I like that idea," Sue said, "only now I wish I hadn't parked under this streetlamp. Let me find a closer spot—one in the dark."

"I'll see if I can book our flights online now," Tanya offered.

CHAPTER TWENTY-TWO

More Trouble

Tanya fetched a luggage trolley from the lobby of the Wyndham and rolled it out to the Pilot, where Ellen and Sue helped her load the three heavy bags before pushing the trolley inside.

Ellen felt like they were being watched, and she resisted the urge to glance around nervously, to avoid appearing suspicious to anyone. Once they were in the room, she was relieved to be reunited with her dog, who seemed just as happy to see her.

"Moseby-Mo! I missed you! Did you miss Mama, too?"

He wiggled his little body and ran between her legs before jumping on the bed to better reach her face, where he kissed her cheeks and chin. She stroked his fur and kissed the top of his head. He was such a comfort to her. She already felt better.

Ellen grabbed his leash from the table. "I need to take him for a walk. Will one of you come with me? My nerves are shot."

Ellen could sense that neither wanted to come. They were both tired, and she didn't blame them. But she wouldn't have asked if she weren't terrified that either John or the Dixie Mafia—or both—might be stalking them.

"I'll go with you," Tanya finally said. "Can we make it quick? I'm tired."

Ellen had little control over how long it would take Mo to do his business, but she said, "We can make it quick, can't we, Moseby-Mo?"

As soon as she clipped on his leash, he made a dash for the door, scratching gently at it—his sign for, "Open, please."

"Okay, okay," she said to him. "Let me get the door open." To Sue, she said, "Lock this door behind us, and don't answer to anyone but us—unless it's the cops and, if it is, make them show their badges."

"Oh, gawd," Sue groaned. "Please hurry it up, girls."

Ellen thrust a plastic bag into her purse and followed Moseby down the hall, with Tanya on her heels. Once they were outside, they walked across the parking lot toward a field of grass. The Waffle House was just across the street from them. They weren't there long when a car crawled up the road toward them.

"Let's go this way, Mo." Ellen tugged at the leash, pulling Mo in the opposite direction of the car.

"Shoot, I'm scared, Ellen. Make him pee, already."

"Sure. I'll just use the power of the Force."

They hurried back to another strip of grass at the entrance to the hotel parking lot, but the car that had crawled down the street between the Waffle House and the Wyndham turned toward them.

"Moseby, if you don't go now, you'll have to hold it," Ellen said irritably.

"Just let him go in the room. It's not worth risking our lives."

"You're right." Ellen tugged Moseby back toward the hotel entrance. "Come on, boy. You had your chance."

As if he knew it was now or never, Mo lifted his leg and peed at the base of the Wingate by Wyndham sign.

"Okay, let's go." Ellen led them back toward the hotel entrance.

She stopped short when the officer who'd questioned them at the convent appeared on foot before the automatic double sliding doors.

"Hello, ladies," the officer greeted. "It's a bit late for a walk, isn't it?"

"Hello, officer," Ellen replied.

Tanya nodded a hello. Ellen avoided making eye contact with Tanya because she already knew what her face looked like.

"We just got here," Ellen said, "as I'm sure you know. My dog had been cooped up for a while."

"Yes, of course."

"Do you have more questions for us?" Ellen asked as she noticed Tanya frantically texting on her phone.

The officer noticed, too. "Who are you texting?"

Tanya blushed. "Sue. I'm just letting her know—"

"Can I see it?"

Tanya's face paled. "What? My phone?"

"Yes. Your phone."

"Um, do I have a choice?"

"Do you have something to hide?"

"No, ma'am. Her you go." Reluctantly Tanya handed it over as tears welled in her eyes.

"Take the doughnut from the bags and hide it," the officer read.

Ellen furrowed her brow at Tanya.

"It's supposed to say hide *them* not *it*," Tanya said quickly. "Clumsy fingers I guess."

The officer lifted her chin and looked down her nose at Tanya, even though Tanya was a half a foot taller. "I don't understand."

"You see, Officer, Ellen wants to lose weight, and our friend Sue bought these bags of doughnuts on the way over. I thought we'd help Ellen out by taking away the temptation."

"How many bags of doughnuts did she buy?" the officer asked.

"Three," Ellen replied. "One for each of us. I was just saying that I'm starving and wanted to eat a whole bag."

"Why take the doughnuts out of the bags?"

"I meant out of the luggage," Tanya clarified. "We were going to pack them and take them to the airport with us for later, for breakfast."

"Where did you buy doughnuts at this hour?" the officer asked.

Ellen glanced at Tanya.

"A convenience store," Tanya said. "I can't remember which one. We picked up those little bags of powdered doughnuts. You know what I'm talking about? Six to a bag?"

"Mm, hmm. They're called a sleeve, not a bag. But you can't recall where you got them?"

Tanya shrugged. "One convenience store looks just like another."

Moseby tugged on his leash toward a spot of grass near the entrance. Ellen walked a few steps away from the officer to let Mo do his business.

The officer followed her. "I noticed you changed your mind."

"What's that, Officer?" Ellen asked. "Changed my mind about what?"

"The luggage in the back of your vehicle. You said you were going to leave it there, since you have an early flight."

"We do have an early flight," Tanya said quickly.

"On second thought, we didn't think it would be safe overnight," Ellen added. "I guess we're a little spooked after that break in on Beach Boulevard."

Ellen fished for the plastic bag in her purse.

"Hands where I can see them, please!" the officer demanded as she reached for her weapon holstered at her waist.

Ellen lifted her hand in the air. "I'm sorry. I was just getting a bag for Mo's poop."

"Leave it for now."

"Alright. Will do, Officer." Ellen's heart was banging on her rib cage now. She wondered, *Geez, when will this end?*

The officer lowered her hand, and Ellen lowered hers.

"Speaking of the break in on Beach Boulevard," the officer began, "we found the other man involved."

"That's great news," Tanya said with a forced smile before glancing nervously at Ellen.

"It seems you know him."

"We do?" Ellen asked, trying to look as dumb and as innocent as she could muster.

"John Fontenot, the homeowner. He was breaking into his own property."

Ellen decided it was better to stop talking. She should have known they weren't going to get away with this. Maybe they should call Trina now.

"It seems you ladies haven't been completely honest with me."

Ellen and Tanya hung their heads. Ellen said a prayer, asking Sister Anna Celeste, Angelique Fayard, Margaret Sherry, and even Mike Gillich for help.

"John Fontenot told us everything—about the money, about the shooting, all of it."

Tanya surprised Ellen by saying, "We didn't mention the money because it wasn't there. We thought it was, but the bag was empty."

"That's interesting. That's what the nuns said, too."

"You spoke with the sisters?" Ellen asked, feeling the blood completely drain from her face.

"Of course, we did. They showed us the empty bag. They said a cat was buried in it, and its remains had likely decomposed to dust. They even quoted the Bible to me, 'for dust thou art, and unto dust shalt thou return.'"

"That's why we didn't say anything about the money," Tanya repeated. "We wanted to make sure it was there before we called you, and when it wasn't, well, what was the point?"

"And the shooting?"

Ellen glanced at Tanya again before saying, "Sue was defending all of us. John had a gun. It was him or us."

"And you failed to tell me this because?"

"We told John that if he left us alone, we wouldn't involve the police," Tanya said. "We were afraid he might still overpower us if we waited for the cops."

"That's an interesting line of thought," the officer said just as a police vehicle pulled up.

The officer behind the wheel—a young, balding man with blond hair and freckles—nodded at the other officer.

The driver parked the vehicle right there in the roundabout in front of the hotel and climbed out.

"My partner has a search warrant from a court of law," the first officer said. "Please show us to your room."

Ellen scooped up Moseby and followed Tanya through the automatic doors of the hotel, through the lobby, and to the elevator. Ellen's knees felt like mush. Tanya's hands were trembling. Ellen wished she'd hide them in her pockets.

When they finally reached their room, Ellen knocked. "Sue, the police are here with a warrant. They want to search the room."

"I'm coming," Sue said, but her voice came from down the hall.

She was carrying an ice bucket full of ice.

"Sorry about that," Sue said as she arrived with the key card. "I wanted some ice for an iced coffee. It's too hot to drink coffee any other way."

Ellen was shocked by how composed Sue appeared as she opened the door for the officers.

"Come on in," Sue said. "Please excuse the mess. I was rearranging things."

Five of their six bags lay opened—two on each bed and one on the floor. Their clothes were half in and half out of them, as if the luggage had been ransacked. Where was their sixth suitcase?

The female officer must have been wondering the same thing. "Is this all the luggage?"

"Yes," Sue replied. "Except for our cosmetic cases, which are on the bathroom counter."

The male officer said, "We're going to need you ladies to sit down over there at that table and stay out of our way while we search the room."

"Of course," Sue said, leading the way. She grabbed a Styrofoam cup, poured some ice in it, and then poured hot coffee over it. "Anyone else want an iced coffee?"

"No, thank you, ma'am," the male officer replied gruffly.

Ellen and Tanya accepted one each and sat with Sue at the little round table while the officers combed through everything. They opened every drawer, took the sheets off the beds, lifted the mattresses, checked beneath the beds, lifted off the couch cushions and opened the sofa bed, checked the closet, and combed through every inch of the restroom.

Ellen was flabbergasted when the police came up empty-handed. Where had Sue hidden the money?

With a tone of frustration, the female officer asked Sue, "So, where are the doughnuts?"

"Excuse me?" Sue's face turned white.

Tanya leaned across the table toward Sue. "You know, the sleeves of powdered doughnuts we bought from that convenient store on the way over?"

"I'll ask the questions, ma'am," the officer barked at Tanya.

"Oh, those," Sue said. "I threw them out—well, I didn't throw them in the trash, that would be wasteful. I gave them to a family with young children. I heard the children crying in the hall as they were passing by our room, and I stuck my head out and asked the parents if they could have them. They didn't speak any English, but they took the doughnuts and went on their way."

"What room are they in?" the officer asked.

"I have no idea," Sue said. "They were passing by. I would think on this floor, but who knows? And I don't know if they were checking in or out. I just wanted the kids to stop crying."

"I think we're done here, Robbins," the male officer said. "You ladies watch yourselves."

Ellen glanced at her friends, wondering what that was supposed to mean. After the officers were gone, Ellen asked, "Was that a threat?"

"Sue, where's the money?" Tanya wanted to know.

"Just wait a while, and I'll show you. Let's make sure they're gone first. In fact, why don't we try to get in some shut-eye before we've got to leave for the airport."

Tanya jumped to her feet. "Are you serious? How on earth can you sleep after all of that?"

"Just tell us where it is," Ellen insisted.

Sue went to the front door and checked through the peephole. Then she opened the door and looked down the hall in each direction before returning to the room.

After locking the door, she returned to the table. "I'm going to whisper, so come close."

Her friends leaned forward.

"I hid it in the other suitcase, and I wedged the suitcase between the ice machine and the wall in the vending room down the hall."

"Genius," Ellen whispered offering Sue a fist to bump. Relief washed over her. Sue had saved the day.

As Sue bumped Ellen's fist, Tanya jumped to her feet again. "Are you saying that there's one point two million dollars hanging out unattended in the vending room?"

Ellen kissed the top of Mo's head. "Calm your horses, Tanya. Better there than here, right?"

"I just saved our hides," Sue complained. "I'd think you'd be grateful. What was that you were saying, Ellen, about me being a genius?"

Tanya took a deep breath and started packing her things back into her suitcase. "I know you're right. If someone steals it, it's still better than us being caught red-handed."

"Exactly," Sue said. "So, we're going to leave it there for a while, in case those cops are still watching us. Why don't we change out of these dirty clothes and try to get a wink?"

Tanya sighed as she stripped off her clothes. "We can try. We've got to be up and out of here in an hour."

"I doubt I'll sleep," Ellen admitted as she kicked off her shoes, "but I wouldn't mind resting in bed for a bit. Who's taking the sofa?"

"I don't mind the sofa," Sue said. "I'm not going to make the bed. I'll just curl up with a blanket and pillow."

As Ellen removed her dirty trousers, she asked Tanya, "So, what was the deal with the doughnuts? That was so stressful and confusing."

Sue found an extra pillow and blanket in the closet. "I was wondering about that, too."

Tanya laughed. "Thank God for autocorrect! I had originally typed, *Take the dough from the bags and hide it!*"

Ellen sank onto the edge of her bed. "I can't believe how close we just came to having our goose cooked for good."

They changed their clothes and turned off the lights. Ellen cuddled with Moseby as her body shuddered with relief. Although she was nervous that the money might not still be there in an hour, she was grateful that she and her friends had avoided arrest. As much as she wanted to help Margaret and Sister Anna Celeste with their unfinished business, she was relieved she wouldn't be going to prison for it.

Not yet, anyway.

Ellen must have dozed off because she was awakened by the sound of the door clicking shut.

She sat up and glared at the door to find Sue returning with the suitcase she had hidden down the hall. Relieved, Ellen fell back on the bed.

"Thank heavens."

"I think what you meant to say was *Thank Sue*."

"Yes, that's exactly what I meant."

"Tanya?" Sue nudged their sleeping friend. "It's time to get a move on. For someone who didn't think she could sleep, you sure did snore loudly."

"Sorry," Tanya said without moving. "Can we *please* take a later flight? I just fell asleep."

"You were snoring for quite a while," Sue insisted. "Come on, we need to get out of Dodge."

Ellen slipped her shoes on and strapped on Mo's cloth pooch carrier. "You think the cops are waiting for us at the airport?"

Sue poured herself another coffee. "I bet they're not finished with us."

"Didn't Priestess Isabel say to cut down on that?" Ellen asked of the coffee.

"Now is not the time, Ellen, so shut it."

"Sorry. Geez."

"I was thinking," Sue began.

"Uh, oh," Ellen interjected. "That's never a good sign."

"You know I saved our hides last night."

"I'm kidding. You were thinking . . ."

"We can't leave this place with one more suitcase than they found on us. We're going to have to leave this one behind."

"Have I told you what a genius you are lately?" Ellen said with a grin.

"Yes, but I don't hear it often enough, so go right ahead."

"You're a genius, Sue."

"I'm glad to finally get some recognition. Now, will you help me distribute this money into the other cases? We can let Tanya sleep a few more winks until we have this sorted."

CHAPTER TWENTY-THREE

The El Reno Correction Facility

It was early November, and Ellen was painting in her backyard studio in San Antonio when she got the call from Trina Gillich. Kirksey Nix had agreed to meet with them.

Ellen had just been thinking about Biloxi, not only because the subject of her painting was the iconic lighthouse, but also because she had just sent her cashier's check for $400,000 to the Sisters of Mercy Orphanage.

"Can you and your friends meet me at the prison on Monday morning around ten o'clock?" Trina asked over the phone.

"We'll be there," Ellen assured her.

Four days later, in El Reno, Oklahoma, Ellen and her friends followed Trina Gillich through a secure gate, down a long corridor, and into a meeting room with tables and chairs secured to the floors. Ellen thought they would have a pane of glass between them and Kirksey Nix, but that wasn't the case. He sat in handcuffs across the table from them only three feet away.

Kirksey Nix appeared to be in his mid-seventies, but his brown, receding hair was less gray than Ellen's roots. He wasn't a large man, except for his medium-sized paunch. His blue eyes were striking, but that was all that was left of a face that, according to photos from the internet, had once been a looker.

After Trina introduced everyone, she tapped on her phone. "I meant to start recording."

"I didn't agree to that," Nix said.

"I don't need your permission," Trina shot back.

"You can't make me talk in here," he said with an easy smile.

"No, you're right," the attractive attorney said, mirroring his same easy smile. "But if you do say something good, I'm sure as hell going to capture it."

"Look at us, just like old friends," the criminal said, still grinning.

"You were my friend, Junior," Trina admitted. "There was a time when you really were my friend. Hell, I think I even had a crush on you. But those days are long gone."

Nix seemed unnerved by Trina's words. His smile faded, he fidgeted with his thumbs, and he sat forward in his chair, leaning on his elbows.

"Why am I here?" he finally asked her.

"These ladies and I experienced something exceptional," Trina began. "They're paranormal investigators, see, and—"

"Did you say *paranormal* investigators?" Nix repeated.

Trina nodded. "That's right."

He looked at Ellen and her friends for the first time, giving them each a curious stare. Ellen glanced down at the table and folded her hands. He scared her to the bone.

"Go on," Nix prompted Trina.

"They talked to my dad." Tears sprang to Trina's eyes and her voice went up an octave. "Junior, I saw him. I saw him with my own eyes."

Nix's eyes widened. "Did he say anything?"

Trina wiped her eyes with the back of her hand. Sue dug a tissue from her purse and handed it over.

"Thanks," Trina said to Sue. Then to Nix, she said, "He called me Tweety Bird, like when I was a little girl. He said it was time for him to go."

"Go where?" Nix asked.

Trina shrugged.

"To the other side," Sue put in. "He's finally at peace."

Nix leaned forward. "Where was he before? In hell or something?" He chuckled as he glanced back at the guard standing in the corner across from them.

"In a way, yes," Sue said. "He was trapped inside the planner that was taken from Vincent Sherry and hidden in the attic of Trina's childhood home."

Nix stared at Sue, apparently speechless.

Feeling a little braver now that Sue had spoken, Ellen piped up, "He's the one who told us to come and talk to you. He wants to save you from experiencing the same torment."

Nix laughed. "Is that right? I think it's a bit late for that, don't you, Trina?"

Recovered from her tears, Trina smiled. "Maybe, but you never know. I think you should hear them out. What could it hurt?"

"Go on, then," he said.

Sue pushed her bangs from her eyes. "Believe it or not, we're not here for ourselves. We made Mike a promise, that's all. And we really do want to help a soul in need."

Nix chuckled again. "You mean me? Am I the soul in need?"

Sue didn't bat an eye. "Yes, Mr. Nix. You are."

He averted his eyes and fidgeted in his seat. "I already got religion. I don't need no holy rollers to come in here and witness to me or anything. I get enough of that in there." He jerked his thumb toward the part of the prison where the cells were located.

"We're not here to convert you," Ellen promised. "Let me get right to the point."

"Please do," Nix insisted.

Ellen took a deep breath. "Mike told us that Pete Halat was never in on the plot to kill the Sherrys."

"Oh, yeah? He said that, huh?"

"He did," Sue said. "He misunderstood you when you said that Pete would pay. He thought you meant he would help pay for the hit."

Nix looked up and seemed to think about that. "You know, that makes sense. I thought *he* said Pete was going to help. I never said it. Well, how about that. All these years, I really did think that Pete was in on it."

Trina lifted her chin. "You never meant to deceive my father about that?"

"No. Why would I?"

"So, Pete would suffer?" Ellen asked.

"I knew Pete was gonna suffer. Vince was his best friend."

Trina raised her brows at Ellen and her friends. "Point one has been corroborated. Let's move on, ladies."

"Does that mean there's a point two?" Nix asked. He looked hard at Tanya. "You, there. You've been awfully quiet. Why don't you tell me if there's a point two?"

Tanya's face turned the color of raspberries. "There is."

"Will you tell it to me, please? I want to hear it from you."

"Leave her alone, Junior. You can't blame her for being nervous around you. You still like that, don't you? Intimidating people?"

Nix laughed.

"I'm not intimidated by you," Sue said. "I feel sorry for you."

"Oh, you do, do you? Well maybe I feel sorry for you."

Ellen prayed that he wouldn't mention her weight, especially now while she was feeling insecure about Tom.

"On to the second point," Trina redirected. "My dad confessed to another murder, and he said you knew about it."

"Which one?" Nix asked with a smile.

Ellen didn't like the man's smug attitude. Unlike Mike Gillich's ghost, Nix showed no remorse for anything.

"Is this a game to you?" Ellen blurted out.

Nix just laughed. "It started out that way. It was a game until it wasn't."

Ellen didn't know what to say.

"Most criminals in here didn't have much of a choice," Nix said with a crooked smile. "They come from poverty or abuse or both. Me, I was different. My family had money. My parents had power. I was restless and bored and got in trouble a lot. At a young age, I could see that respect, power, and money would be easier had through crime. I also learned that things didn't have to end behind bars. Hell, I ran my best scam from Angola Prison. It was a fun ride. And you know what? There's not a whole lot I regret. I took advantage of the scum of the earth. I preyed on evildoers—people who gambled their money away and used and abused women *and* men. Those homosexuals got what they deserved, thinking they could take advantage of someone vulnerable behind bars just by giving over their money. They were despicable. Everyone I ever scammed or killed was despicable. I never touched the innocent. That's why Trina was my friend. She was a good girl. I left her alone."

Trina closed her eyes and shook her head, the disapproval apparent.

"You still a good girl, Trina?" he asked.

She met his gaze but did not match his smile. "Back to point two."

"Yes, tell me. I'm listening."

Trina turned to Sue.

Sue cleared her throat. "Mike Gillich confessed to killing Sister Anna Celeste. He said you knew about it. He wanted you to admit that you knew about it."

"I didn't condone it, but I didn't talk him out of it, either. Mike had got word that the nun was hiding my money. Never knew if it was true."

"So, you admit my father murdered the nun, and that you knew about it?" Trina asked.

"Yes. Please tell me there's a point three." He turned to Tanya. "Is there a point three?"

Tanya shook her head.

Trina stopped the recording and returned her phone to her bag before standing up. "Thanks, Junior. You take care of yourself in here."

Ellen and her friends stood up, too.

"Don't leave yet, ladies. We were just getting to know each other. Isn't there a point three?"

Trina ignored him and went to the guard. Ellen and her friends followed.

"Come on, Trina! Don't leave yet. I'm not done talking to you!" Nix's pleas became desperate.

As Ellen followed Trina and her friends down the corridor of the prison, she could still hear Nix crying out to them to stay.

Two days later, Trina sent Ellen and her friends a video of a local reporter who had taken an interview with Trina. The reporter, a brunette in her forties with large-framed glasses and a pretty smile, said, "In an ironic twist of events, Trina Gillich, daughter of Mike Gillich, once known as the godfather of Biloxi, secured a confession from Kirksey Nix, Jr., co-conspirator in the 1987 murders of Vincent and Margaret Sherry. Nix confessed that former mayor Pete Halat was not involved in the murder for hire. Nix also revealed that Gillich was responsible for the death of a local beloved nun, Sister Anna Celeste of the Sisters of Mercy Convent, who was found dead in her bed a week after the Sherrys deaths for what was, at the time, believed to be natural causes. Nix said that they'd heard a rumor that the nun was hiding the stolen money from the Halat and Sherry law firm, which was the impetus for the tragic events that followed. Nix said the rumor was never proved to be true and so the disappearance of the money remains a mystery to this day."

CHAPTER TWENTY-FOUR

Return to Biloxi

In her backyard studio on a beautiful day in early December, Ellen stepped back from her painting to have a better look. She compared her rendition of the lighthouse to the Christmas ornament she had purchased over the summer while visiting Biloxi. In addition to its pleasing structure and the gentle waves of the gulf behind it, Ellen had wanted to portray the shadowy image of Angelique Fayard standing on the observation deck looking over her land. Satisfied, Ellen declared the painting finished.

She had just put her brushes into the sink to soak when she heard Moseby barking in the yard outside.

Poking her head through the door, she asked, "What's the matter, Moseby-Mo?"

Tanya and Ellen were walking up the drive to her backyard gate.

Ellen stepped from her studio to meet them. "Well, hello, girlfriends."

Sue handed her a small Panera Bread bag. "We brought you a cookie."

It was a shortbread cookie—Ellen's favorite.

"How thoughtful. Thank you. What are you girls up to?"

Tanya gave her a half-smile. "We didn't want to bother you while you were in your painting mode, but we wanted you to know that we were thinking of you."

"Aw. That's so sweet. Well, I just finished. Want to see it?"

"Oh, goodie," Sue said in a way that Ellen wasn't sure was sincere. "Yes. Let's see it."

"Hi, Moseby," Tanya greeted as Ellen opened the gate to the backyard.

Moseby wiggled his body and ran between each of their legs before they were able to make it past him to the studio door.

Before they went inside, Sue said, "Oh, I want to tell you something first, something really sweet that Tom said to me."

Ellen glanced at Tanya. "I'm all ears."

"Well, I asked him how he'd feel about renewing our vows."

"What did he say?"

"He said you only renew things that expire. He said our vows are forever."

Ellen lifted her arms and wrapped them around her friend. "That *was* a sweet thing to say. I told you he wasn't having an affair."

"Well, for once, you were right." Then Sue added, "Though, Tom might have felt differently if charges had been brought against me for shooting John Fontenot."

Ellen shook her head and laughed and led them into her studio. "I'm just glad that's behind us. Didn't Trina say John and his brother-in-law were already out on probation?"

"Yep, that's right," Tanya confirmed. "Hopefully, they learned their lesson. I know I learned mine."

"Would you have done things in Biloxi differently?" Ellen asked.

Tanya shrugged. "I don't know. I'm glad the orphanage benefited. And I'm glad Margaret and Sister Anna Celeste can finally rest."

Once inside, Sue said, "Oh, Ellen. It's gorgeous."

Tanya nodded. "I really love it. You really captured Biloxi."

"Speaking of Biloxi," Sue began, "Tanya has some news."

Tanya's smile split her face in half. "That's right. I'm a Biloxi homeowner."

Ellen's mouth dropped open. "What? What are you talking about?"

"Well, I guess since I'm the one who booked our summer house rental, I received a notification about a week ago that it was going on the market. I immediately called Dave's mom's real estate agent and asked her to write up an offer. It was accepted this morning."

Ellen gaped. "You bought the house on Beach Boulevard?"

"Want to help me fix it up?"

Ellen looked at Sue and then turned her gaze back to Tanya, trying to take it all in. "Of course! But why didn't you keep me in the loop about this?"

Tanya flapped a hand through the air. "I hate bothering you when you're painting."

"You're never a bother! How many times do I have to tell you guys that! Oh, my gosh! How soon can we get started?"

Sue put a hand on her hip. "Could you be ready to go next week? That's when Tanya closes on the house."

Ellen snapped her fingers. "That would be perfect. You know why? I was planning to buy Christmas gifts for the Biloxi orphans this year. I asked Sister Martha for a list. Anyway, wouldn't it be fun to deliver the gifts in person?"

"I've been wanting to check out the expansion," Tanya said. "The photos Sister Martha emailed us are just, wow, I mean, she's managed to make a lot of improvements in a relatively short time."

"Then it's settled," Sue declared. "We'll go to Biloxi next week to see the orphanage, deliver presents, and begin renovations on Tanya's new summer house."

"I'm thinking it might make a better winter house," Tanya said. "I'll rent it in the summers and use it in the winters. Wouldn't that be nice?"

"I guess we're about to find out for ourselves what winter's like in Biloxi," Ellen said, clapping her hands. "I can't wait to eat at Mary Mahoney's again."

"That's all I ever think about anymore," Sue admitted.

Ellen lifted a finger. "And I just thought of something, Tanya. You won't hurt my feelings if you don't want it, but wouldn't my painting look perfect over the mantle on the third floor of your new house?"

Tanya's hands flew to her cheeks. "Are you serious? That would be amazing!"

"Then it's settled," Sue said. "I'll call the sisters and let them know we're coming."

Tanya clapped her hands, too. "I'll book our flights. I'm so excited."

"Oh, I almost forgot," Ellen said suddenly. "A man from Salt Lake City wants to hire Brian and his brother to renovate an old cabin on an island in the Great Salt Lake. He wants to turn it into a bed and breakfast. Brian and his brother are swamped and want to know if we'll take it on. He wants the job done this summer. Do you think we can manage both renovations?"

"How fun!" Sue said. "I would think we could manage that. What do you think, Tanya?"

"We just have the top floor at my house to worry about. It shouldn't take long. I'd love to go to Utah."

"Well, there's one more thing," Ellen said with a mischievous grin. "The bridge that once joined the island to the mainland is rumored to be haunted."

"What?" Tanya and Sue said together, both wearing smiles.

"We might have to do a little ghost healing while we're there," Ellen said. "Are y'all up for that?"

"I'm always up for that," Sue declared. "Tanya?"

"Let's do it!"

***

THE END

Thank you for reading my story. I hope you enjoyed it! If you did, please consider leaving a review. Reviews help other readers to discover my books, which helps me.

Please visit my website at evapohler.com to get the next book, *The Haunted Bridge.*

EVA POHLER

Eva Pohler is a *USA Today* bestselling author of over thirty novels in multiple genres, including mysteries, thrillers, and young adult paranormal romance based on Greek mythology. Her books have been described as "addictive" and "sure to thrill"—*Kirkus Reviews*.

To learn more about Eva and her books, and to sign up to hear about new releases and sales, please visit her website at https://www.evapohler.com.

Acknowledgments

I would like to thank these premium members for their continual support:

Tiffani Adams
Charli Callanan
Kristi Chambers
Theresa Christ
Rebekka and Sherry Colegrove
Amanda Ecker
Kerry Erickson
Jessica Garza
Samie Hall-Rood
Kanyon Kiernan
Misty Killion
Anita Klaboe
Kimberly Landry
Leslie Lawrence
Linda Lemelin
Chris Ann Livingston
Samantha Lundergan
Carrie McCauley
Glorianna Murry
Carrington Parker
Liana Petrone
Rachel Renzo
Candy Smith
Kristi Van Howling

Made in the USA
Middletown, DE
06 October 2023

40346395R00136